A Demon
on the Lion Bridge

An Abby Renshaw Supernatural Mystery

Jack Massa

 Triskelion Books

Published by
Triskelion Books
www.triskelionbooks.com

This is a work of fiction. All of the characters, organizations, and events portrayed in this novel are either products of the author's imagination or are used fictitiously.

A Demon on the Lion Bridge
Copyright © 2023 by Jack Massa

ISBN: 978-0-9976461-9-1

Print Edition published February, 2023

Cover design by Shaun Stevens, https://www.flintlockcovers.com/

For Vicki-Marie Petrick

and Angelisa Fontaine-Wood,

two of the best writers I know!

1. The Demon Vanishes

Running in sunshine, nearing the top of the Bridge of Lions, I think how lovely the sky and water look, how lucky I am to have landed my summer internship here in St. Augustine.

Then my mind flips back to the 5K I'm running. I'm somewhere in the middle of the pack, surrounded by runners of various ages, and by spectators lining the sidewalks on the two-lane bridge.

And I'm sucking wind. Because it's freaking hot in St. Augustine, even at the end of May. But mostly, I have to admit, because I've let my conditioning lapse.

I can still finish with a decent time if I just focus. Ariel is somewhere ahead. He's driven up from Orlando for the Memorial Day Weekend, to run in the race and visit with me. We used to do running club together in college. Back then, my fitness was a lot better. I really don't want him thinking I've turned into a slug.

I push harder as I near the summit of the bridge.

That's when I see the demon.

It stands by the rail behind the spectators. The thing must be seven or eight feet tall: with round bulky shoulders, long thick arms, dark orange skin that glistens like oil in the sun. It looks exactly like a demon from some comic book or fantasy game, right down to the curved horns and fiery red eyes.

I pull up in shock. The runner behind jostles me, a man with gray hair, scowling as he turns sideways to get around me. I stumble to the edge of the road. The demon has noticed me now and is staring.

Damn! I'm supposed to be running a road race here. Not a good time to be visited by a weird psychic vision—or whatever this is.

The demon curls its lips in a smile.

Then it vanishes.

~~~

It takes a few seconds to get my head back into the race. Definitely won't finish with one of my better times today.

Hard to think about that after spotting an evil entity messing up the beautiful view.

I merge back into the flow of racers. Shoes striking the pavement, I run down the long, gentle slope of the bridge.

I have to admit I'm baffled. Oh, I've dealt with supernatural beings before—thought-forms, entities conjured by magic, even a mythical goddess or two. It all started when I was twelve: hallucinations of alligator people and monsters from online games. My mom sent me to a psychiatrist, and when they put me on anxiety meds it all went away—for a while. Then, at the end of my junior year in high school, it came back, big time: ghosts and a slimy swamp monster. That's what led me back to Florida, and Harmony Springs where my grandma lives. That's where I discovered my family heritage of *true magic*. Among other things, I learned that what I had believed to be insane hallucinations were real—spirits and manifestations from other realms.

So seeing apparitions is old news for me. But a *demon*, in the bright sunshine on an historic bridge in St. Augustine?

That's too weird.

At the foot of the bridge I pass the two marble lions, run around the traffic circle, and head for the finish line. The 5K is a charity event, part of the city's Memorial Day festivities. A crowd is gathered in the historic plaza, cheering the runners. After passing under the finish-line banner, I check my time, then walk over to the grass. Bending over, I put my hands on my knees and suck in air.

"How did you do, Abby?" Ariel places a hand on my shoulder.

I look up at him and smile. He's a bit taller than me, with a runner's physique, black hair and soft brown eyes. I met him my first year of college at Claremont State. We got to be close friends. Besides running club we did other things together. For a while, we were even in a relationship. But that didn't last.

"Over thirty-five minutes," I tell him, frowning. "How about you?"

"Not bad. Just under twenty-nine. You feel okay?"

"Yeah. Need to get in better shape though, obviously."

I consider telling Ariel about the demon. Well, because the *other things* we've done together include studying different magical traditions, plus a couple of supernatural adventures. But by now I've convinced myself the demon was just some stray apparition and will probably amount to nothing. I don't want to spoil Ariel's holiday by bringing it up.

"Still on for lunch?" he asks.

"Sure."

I take out my phone, and we compare notes on restaurants. We select one called *Barnacles*, on the edge of the historic district and across the street from the river. It has an upstairs dining room with a great view.

It's just after 11 a.m., and we agree to meet at one. That will give us both time to shower and change. Ariel gives me a hug (sweaty as we both are) and walks off toward his hotel. I take another minute to collect myself, then head back toward the river.

I'm renting a tiny apartment in a house on Dumas Street, a fifteen-minute walk from the Bridge of Lions. It would be a little quicker to cut through the neighborhood south of the plaza, but something draws me back to the water.

Maybe it's the views. Avenida Menendez winds along the riverfront, past ancient brick buildings that house storefronts and restaurants. Across the road is a narrow park with palms, curved walks, and docks where sailboats ride at anchor. Sometimes you can see dolphins out on the water.

As I'm nearing the corner of Bridge Street, I spot a young woman sitting on a concrete wall. She's blond, slim, and looks about my age. Beside her stands a pelican, perched on the wall with wings spread.

Now, pelicans are not a rare sight here. But you don't usually see one so close to a human. Weirder still, it looks like this girl is *talking* to the pelican—as in, holding a friendly and meaningful conversation.

I stop to watch from the other side of the street. Maybe it wasn't just the views that made me pick this route. Maybe some psychic business is afoot, and this is part of it.

The girl notices me watching and frowns.

While we peer at each other, the air in front of the girl wavers. A red mist spouts from the ground. It widens and spirals and then, in the mist, the demon appears.

He looks exactly as he did on the bridge—massive, gleaming, and terrible—as he gazes down at the girl.

She jumps to her feet. *She can see the demon too.*

But she doesn't turn and run.

Instead, she peers at it for a long moment. I get the feeling she's seen this thing before.

Still facing the monster, she takes a step to the side. Then she waves at the pelican—like telling it goodbye—turns, and marches away.

The demon stares after her. Then his head swivels and he spots me across the road.

I stand straighter, not flinching, making the point that I'm not afraid. Well, at least trying to convince the demon of that.

We look at each other for a moment. Then my eyes shift back to the girl. She glances at me, then behind her at the demon, as she hurries on.

When I look back, the pelican has flown away.
Once again, the demon has vanished.

2. Does that mean what I think it means?

As I walk the narrow back streets of St. Augustine, passing houses and inns hundreds of years old, I think about the demon.

What kind of spirit is it? The fact that it literally looks like a horned monster from a fantasy game is not a good sign. What does it portend? What did it mean that the girl saw it too? Was she really talking to the pelican?

Or am I just having random visions projected from my unconscious, waking nightmares caused by anxiety? That's a simpler explanation, and maybe the more likely. Certainly, I have been under a lot of stress lately. Just over two weeks ago, I moved to St. Augustine and started my internship at the law office. Living here on my own, my first professional job—huge steps out into the big, scary world. And it was anxiety, at age twelve, that triggered my first psychic visions—or "hallucinations" as the psychiatrist called them. And this demon sure looks like one of the crazy things I saw back then.

Except Violet, my magical mentor, later told me that even those early experiences were at some level real. She explained that I'm naturally psychic and see things other people don't. More often than not, my visions are not simply projections from my personal unconscious, but from the *collective* unconscious—or else from spirit realms beyond. Often, they mean something important.

So, right now, I don't know what to think.

I turn the corner onto Dumas Street. My apartment is an efficiency on the third floor of a white Victorian-era house. I trudge up the wood stairs on the outside of the building, take out my key and unlock the door.

Peeking inside, I scan the apartment.

No sign of any spirits. Good.

Stepping inside, I shut the door and lean my back against it. I take some deep breaths to center myself.

I'm planning to spend the day with Ariel, sight-seeing. This should be fun for both of us. I determine to push all demon thoughts out of my mind.

〰〰

Our table in the upstairs dining room gives a splendid view of the waterfront. The ruins of the old Spanish fort lie to our left, the Bridge of Lions a block to the right. Across the Mantanzas River, Anastasia Island lies dark green under the brilliant sky. Boats cruise back and forth, and sea gulls and pelicans fly overhead.

Showered, hair washed, dressed in nice shorts and blouse, I feel much better. I sip sparkling water and watch Ariel across the table.

He's telling me about his job. He works as a junior accountant in Orlando, at a branch office of a firm based in Miami. The work is demanding and requires lots of extra hours. Which is why I was surprised when he got in touch to tell me he was taking a long weekend to visit St. Augustine. Partly to run the 5K, but also because he wanted to see me. First time we've been together in over a year— since he graduated college last May.

While telling me about his life in Orlando, he hasn't mentioned any girlfriends. I wonder if it might be in the back of his mind to relight our old romance.

Staring at his soft brown eyes, I wonder how I'd feel about that.

"But tell me about you, Abby. How do you like St. Augustine so far?"

"Well, the city is amazing, of course. I'm looking forward to taking in the sights with you today."

"And your job at the law office?"

"Okay, so far. I've sat in on meetings and done research. The people are nice, but it's a little intimidating."

He picks up his beer glass and grins. "Abby intimidated? That's hard for me to imagine."

"Well, the Law is all about knowledge and precedent, being exact and careful. So I worry about making mistakes."

"Pressure. I get it," Ariel says. "From what I understand, most law interns are either already in law school, or have at least finished undergrad work. So you having this position is a bit unusual, no?"

He's right. I still have a year left in college. "Yeah. To be honest, my mom pulled a few strings. She's an investment banker up in New York, you know?"

"Oh. I thought she worked in London."

"She used to. She got promoted last year and transferred back to the main office. Anyway, me getting an internship this summer was her idea. She suggested New York or New Jersey, but I insisted I wanted to stay near Harmony Springs and my grandma. Mom asked around with her partners and clients and found Sheldon and Bond here in St. Augustine."

He nods, smiling. "Your mother knows people who know people. It's the same way in the business community. My dad's cousin helped me find my present job."

The server brings out plates, Tilapia and salad for me, a Cuban sandwich and fries for Ariel. We dig in, and the conversation drifts to the delicious food and the beautiful view and what places we're going to tour this afternoon.

Then Ariel asks me: "What about your magical work? Anything new with that?"

When we met my freshman year, along with running club, Ariel was a leader in a "Postmodern Magic" study group on campus. I worked for a while with that group, and later I introduced Ariel to the Circle of Harmony. That's the magical order based in Harmony Springs, created by the founders of the town in the late 1800s. Ariel became keen on it and initiated. So, for a time, we were both following two separate magical paths.

But magic takes a lot of work, and with all the distractions in our lives, over time it seems we've both focused on it less.

"Not much," I admit. "I still meditate and do rituals to keep in balance. That much is essential for me. But not much studying. Just haven't had the time. What about you?"

He lowers his eyes, looking forlorn. "Same. I haven't been back to Harmony Springs in a couple of years. Are Violet and Kevin and your grandmother still practicing?"

"Oh yeah. They still do the Circle of Harmony rituals at the solstices and equinoxes. I attend when I'm there. The energy's not as strong as it used to be, though. Violet's been ill, on and off, you know?"

"I am sorry to hear that. I really should visit them some time." He puts down his sandwich, gazes at the plate. After a pause, he says, "I miss the magic, Abby. That first year after we met, there was so much energy. Those adventures we had—not always easy, but we made it through them and … I really felt I was making progress in the spirit realms, discovering new possibilities everywhere. But I got busier and busier with school and work and now … I don't know. I wonder if I'm not turning into my parents. Do you ever feel that way?"

Well, that's a different kind of scary thought. Ariel is searching my face. I have to admit I can relate to what he's saying. I haven't given up on the magical path, but life in the so-called "real world" can be so demanding.

"I don't know. It's hard to do everything and—Oh!"

I've looked across the room and locked eyes with a young woman standing behind the bar. She's staring at me, and after an instant I realize who she is.

The girl I spotted at the dock, with the pelican and the demon.

She looks away. I frown.

"Something wrong?" Ariel turns to look over his shoulder.

"No, I—" The girl is going about her business, tending bar. *Probably not the same girl at all. Probably just my imagination ...*

"What were we talking about? Oh, right ... I do feel that way, sometimes, Ariel. But college is hard and law school is going to be harder, and a person only has so much energy. You have to make choices. I haven't given up on my magical training, but I have put it on a back burner. That's just a choice I had to make, for now."

He nods, his eyes wistful. "So you don't think my pursuing of magic was just youthful folly?"

"Positively not! And I believe there'll be plenty more magic to explore, whenever you feel ready." I pick up my fork. "Now, let's finish our delicious lunch and then go out and view the sites in this beautiful city, and enjoy ourselves."

〜〜〜

We spend the afternoon touring the most touristy sites of the old city: the Castillo de San Marcos, the Pirate Museum, the Ponce de Leon Fountain of Youth. Ariel serves as guide. He's traced his ancestry back to the early Spanish settlers of St. Augustine, and he knows the city well. For me, it's all new and lots of fun—except that I sense a lingering sadness in him, like he's missing something in his life.

Around six, we end up back at his hotel. He's booked a room at the *Casa Lucia*, right across from the city plaza. It's a big, gorgeous building that dates back to the late eighteen hundreds, St. Augustine's "gilded age."

"I can't believe you're staying here," I tell him. "Gotta be the most expensive hotel in town."

Ariel lifts a shoulder. "I'm making good money. It's okay to spend a little."

He asks if I'd like something to eat. Neither of us is hungry, so we end up sitting in the lobby and ordering drinks: ginger ale for me, a beer for him. Between the 5K and all the touring, we're both tired out. The conversation lapses as we sip from our glasses. But that's okay. It's nice to relax on the plush sofa and just rest and—and be with someone you're comfortable with.

Gazing around, I appreciate the woodwork, the chandeliers, the beautiful rugs. "This place is gorgeous!"

Ariel smiles. "The room they gave me is equally impressive. Splendid view of the city." His expression turns serious. "How would you feel if I invited you up to my room?"

Does that mean what I think it means? I search his eyes. *Yes. It does.* How would I feel? Honest answer: "Touched. Scared. Not sure I should."

Ariel nods. "I understand, Abby. Is it still Ray-Ray?"

"No ... "

Ray-Ray was my first love. I met him that first summer in Harmony Springs. When I met Ariel, Ray-Ray and I had broken up. But then we got back together. For a while, I tried to carry on a relationship with both of them. That proved a disaster, so I broke it off with both. Until my fickle heart decided I really did love Ray-Ray, and we got back together yet again. For six months or so, that went great. Then it didn't.

Anyway, Ray-Ray left Harmony Springs after he graduated college last year. He's living up in Washington now, training with the FBI.

"... Ray-Ray and I haven't been together since we broke up. I mean, for the third time."

"That was two years ago," Ariel says. "Is there someone else?"

"No. Frankly, I haven't wanted to try. When I was with you guys, I ended up being hurt, and hurting both of you. Maybe I'm just not cut out for relationships."

Ariel's quiet for a moment. "I don't believe that, Abby. I don't think you really do either."

Really not sure what I believe. "Well, at least for now, with all the other pressures I'm under, I can't go there." I touch his hand on the table. "I love you as a friend, Ariel. I always will. I'm sorry."

He squeezes my hand, then lets it go. "Well. Can't blame a guy for trying. At least let me walk you home. That's the gentlemanly thing to do."

3. Now, this one is different

Back at my apartment, on the landing outside door, I hug Ariel and wish him a safe journey home.

As I watch him walk down the steps in the twilight, a feeling of sadness creeps up on me. Was it a mistake not to spend the night with him?

No. With all the complications in my life right now: living on my own, law internship, law school applications looming—not to mention demonic visions—how could I possibly handle a romance? Especially a long-distance romance?

Back at the restaurant, Ariel and I talked about how we both lack the time and attention to devote to magical study. But now I'm thinking: if there's no room in my life for spiritual work, and no room for love, then what's it all for?

Am I making the wrong decisions?

Ugh!

Stepping inside, I check the apartment carefully for evil manifestations. Finding none, I strip off my clothes and take a long shower. The hot water relaxes me and makes me realize how utterly tired I am.

Well, I *did* run a 5K this morning. After training hardly at all. Not to mention everything else that happened today.

I put on a nightgown and crawl into bed. I read a few law case reviews on my tablet, but that just makes me drowsier. Soon, I drift off to sleep.

〰

Some of the weirdest stuff happens in my dreams.

I'm inside a tower, climbing a spiral staircase made of black iron. A circle of sunlight beams far overhead. I'm desperately rushing up there. Something urgent I need to do.

But my body's exhausted—because I've let my conditioning lapse. But also because I'm terrified.

I drag myself to the top and stumble through a doorway. A steel floor lies under my feet, and I grab onto a railing. Looking around, I see a spectacular view of the coast—flat land, bridges, water blazing in the sunshine. St. Augustine lies in the distance. I know this place: the top of the lighthouse on Anastasia Island.

But I'm not alone. Around the curve of the landing, I see the demon. He's seated on the rail, his back to empty air. With him are two others.

One is the blond girl I saw with the pelican (and again, maybe, later at the bar). She's wearing a nightie and standing stiff, arms hanging at her sides. *Enthralled.*

Behind her stands a guy, heavy and bearded and dressed in a wizard's robe—like some character straight out of a fantasy game.

I stand frozen. The demon glances at me and points a clawed finger. He addresses the wizard in a creepy whisper.

"Another has arrived. She will wait." He points to the blond girl. "Now, fix your attention on this one."

The wizard guy nods eagerly. He pulls a smartphone out of his robe and points the camera. The demon faces the blond girl.

"You love birds, I know. You love them so much, you would like to be a bird."

Her arms shudder. A gasp escapes her throat. "No!"

"Oh, yes," says the demon. "You would love to fly. You have wings, like a seagull ..."

Breathing hard, the girl takes a step toward the rail. Then another. I can feel the dread pulsing from her. I strain to move, but I'm helpless.

The demon smiles. The wizard watches, awestruck, like he's recording the best video ever.

"No!" The girl climbs onto the lower rung of the railing. Her shins press the upper rail, her arms spread wide, trembling. I'm breathing in her terror like a vapor.

And, I realize, so are the demon and the wizard.

"Now spread your wings, young woman!" the demon cries. "Spread your seagull wings and fly!"

Her body pitches forward. The horrible scream fades as she plummets toward the ground.

After a quiet moment, the demon turns and peers at me. "Now," he says to the wizard. "This one is different."

∿

My eyes pop open, staring at the ceiling over my bed. My room's on the top floor, and beams meet high up at the top of the gable. Plenty of room up there for shadowy monsters to lurk, so I stare for a long time, breathing hard, waiting for my heartbeat to slow.

That dream was creepy as hell. And it means that the demon— even if he is a product of my anxious imagination—is still with me.

I seriously need a psychic housecleaning.

When I'm calm enough, I stand and do long, gentle stretches. Then I sit cross-legged on the bed and start the Daily Ablution. This is a basic grounding ritual, the first exercise taught in the Circle of Harmony. There are five Springs (or Fountains) of Harmony, named for the actual springs near the town. With my eyes shut, I visualize each Spring pouring into the nerve centers on my spine: first the Spring of Love at the root, next Endurance at the solar plexus ...

Often during this exercise, I slip into trance. Sometimes I meet spirits who give me messages or guidance. When the water rises to my heart center, representing the Spring of Balance, I see a silver fountain with two basins, water pouring gently from one to the other. Beside the fountain stands a lady dressed in shining robes, with a square headdress and wings. A lion lies peacefully at her feet.

I've met her before, but not for a long time. She is the ancient Mesopotamian goddess Inanna.

Three years ago, I was drawn into a quest to obtain certain magical drawings called *sigils*. These sigils had been created by magicians in the early 20th Century. They were students of ancient civilizations, interested in the old gods. These particular sigils were designed to evoke Inanna's power. During my quest, I encountered the goddess in a vision. She named me then as her priestess.

After that adventure, I planned to study sigil magic and cultivate my relationship with Inanna. But that's another magical path I've failed to explore, despite my good intentions. In the past couple of years, I've only glimpsed the goddess a few times.

Now, in the vision, I bow and greet her with one of her ancient titles. "Hail to the Lady who lights the morning and evening sky."

Her eyes shift and she stares down at me. I think she's about to speak.

But, after a moment, she and the lion fade like shadows.

Now I'm confused. Did this happen because I'm so out of practice with my magical work? Did Inanna have something to tell me, but my brain's too out-of-tune to receive it? Why did she appear at all? Does it have something to do with the demon?

I take a deep breath and finish the Ablution. The water rises from my heart to the throat center, where I envision the Spring of Amity, then to the top of my head, and the Spring of Bliss. I let the waters of Bliss pour like a waterfall over my body, cleansing my aura.

When it's done I feel steadier, but not exactly relaxed.

More like troubled and confused.

~~~

I sleep poorly the rest of the night. When the alarm on my phone buzzes at seven, I roll over, achy and groggy. But I have to work today, so I hoist myself out of bed, put on the coffee pot, then slump around getting dressed.

I've just poured coffee when I hear an incoming ringtone. I see it's my grandma, so I answer right away.

"Abby? Hope I didn't wake you. Are you doing okay?"

Well ... I consider confiding something of the current state of my life. Grandma is herself a true magician and knows about my various supernatural troubles and triumphs. But there's not a lot she could do to help me at the moment. Also, I don't have much time to talk.

"I'm okay, Grandma. How are you?"

"Oh. Fine. I wouldn't have called but I had a—well, call it a premonition, that you might be having trouble."

"Nothing to speak of at the moment. How are you doing?"

"Oh, same old same old. We all miss you, you know? Violet's been ill again, I'm afraid. She just can't seem to shake the effects of that virus."

Violet is the leader of our circle and has taught me much of what I know about magic. She's in her late seventies and has been in fragile health for some years now. Last winter, a bad virus went around and put her in the hospital with pneumonia. She's also on blood pressure medicine, but doesn't always remember to take it—or else doesn't like to take it because of how it makes her feel.

"I'm sorry to hear that. Please give her my love when you see her."

"I will."

"How are you feeling, Grandma?"

"Oh, fine. Business is picking up at the shop now that summer's here."

"Are you holding up okay?" The last few years, I've helped Grandma with her antique shop in downtown Harmony Springs, especially in the summers. Now that I'm living out of town, I've been a little worried about how she'll manage. She's close to seventy herself.

"Oh, it's fine. There might actually be some news on that front."

"What kind of news?"

"Well, nothing definite. We'll talk about it later. I know you need to get ready for work."

I check the clock. "Yeah ..."

"You're sure you're okay though, sweetie?"

Glancing around the corners of the room, I answer. "Sure, Grandma. Don't worry about me."

4. The place of slaughter

The Law Offices of Sheldon and Bond are on a narrow street on the northern edge of the historic district, a mile and a half from my apartment. I get there at 8:25 and park my Mazda in the tiny parking lot on the side. I'm dressed in skirt and blouse and nice sandals, my hair up and a conservative amount of makeup. Checking the mirror, I verify that, despite my lack of sleep, I look professional and at least semi-alert.

The building is a mid-size Victorian house built in the 1870s, with steep roofs and a wraparound porch. Except for the sign out front, you'd never know it was an office. The firm handles all kinds of business and real estate law. My ambition is to eventually focus on environmental law, but this is still a great learning opportunity for my first internship.

In addition to the two partners, Larry Sheldon and Teresa Bond, there's a paralegal, Nancy, and the office manager, Gloria. It's the start of my third week here and everyone has been kind to me. They've never employed an intern before, and at first they didn't quite know what to do with me. Mostly, I've been reviewing contracts, briefs, and correspondences from their files, and discussing the cases with Nancy or one of the attorneys. Larry said that this week he would assign me to write the first draft of a property sales agreement for a new client.

The offices occupy only the first floor of the converted Victorian home, so there's not a lot of space. They set up a small table for me in a corner of the file room. No windows, unfortunately.

After checking in with Gloria and Nancy, I spend the next couple of hours in my little corner, reading case files and making notes. The real estate contracts are pretty standard stuff and, given that I'm sleep-deprived, I struggle to keep my mind on the work. I remedy this with more coffee.

At eleven, the whole team gathers in the conference room for a staff meeting. The two attorneys sit at the heads of the table. Teresa is a Black lady in her early forties, short-haired and slim, dressed in a navy blue suit. Larry's younger and a little less formal, tall and slightly overweight, wearing a tan sports coat today. Gloria the office manager sits next to me, a stout woman in her fifties, prim and professional. Nancy, the paralegal, sits across from us, wearing a light gray suit. She's in her late twenties or early thirties and always looks polished and self-contained.

There are currently five cases in the works, and the attorneys review and discuss them one by one. Gloria and I both take minutes. I'm allowed to ask questions, and occasionally they even add comments to make sure I'm grasping a particular point.

I'm following along fine until halfway through the meeting. Out of the corner of my eye, I glimpse a shadow pass in front of the big picture window. I blink and look up from my keyboard.

My vision shivers. The oily orange-skinned beast stands in the corner, smiling at me. My mouth drops open and I stare, pushing down a squeak of terror.

"Abby? You okay?"

Shaking, I gape at Teresa. Everyone is looking at me. *How long was I frozen?* Of course, no one else can see the demon.

"Abby?" Nancy touches my elbow.

"Oh! Sorry. Forgive me. My mind wandered for a moment."

Hands back to the keys, Abby. Stare at the screen, not at the creepy spirit.

Desperately, I attune my mind to following the legal discussions. I avoid looking back at that corner until the meeting breaks up.

By which time the demon is gone.

〜〜〜

This is getting serious. Creeping me out in my dreams is one thing. Interrupting me at work is something else. If this monster isn't going away on his own, I'll have to get rid of him.

Something I am perfectly capable of doing.

... I hope.

First, I need to understand as best I can the nature of the demon—what it is and where it comes from. I'm tempted to use he/him pronouns for the critter, but that's just an assumption. No assumptions allowed. I need to see, as clearly as possible, the truth.

In Circle of Harmony magic, that means using the *seeing stone.*

The stone is one of four tools you make on the path of true magic. Each tool corresponds to one of the first four Springs: wand for Love, dagger for Endurance, seeing stone for Balance, cup for Amity. As you advance in the order, you master the powers of each Spring, and earn the tools like badges of the grades. There is no tool associated with the final Spring, Bliss, which represents the culmination of the path.

In my first two years of study, I had occasion to make each of the tools and advance to all five of the grades. So, literally speaking, I qualify as an adept.

Yeah, right.

I mean, at times I have wielded some pretty potent magic, and a few times I've felt pretty accomplished. But at this point I'm so out of practice that I'm not feeling at all "adept."

Time to up my game again.

As soon as I get home that evening, without bothering about dinner, I go to the closet and sort through my luggage for my magical gear. Wand, dagger, cup, and seeing stone, I lay them out on the table that serves as my desk, along with a candle and some incense.

I sit in the chair with my back straight, take a few deep breaths, then light the candle and set fire to the incense. With them burning, I pick up the seeing stone—a faceted topaz set in silver, with a silver chain I can wear as a necklace. I inherited the stone from Thomas Renshaw, my great, great grandfather, one of the original Founders of the Circle.

Holding the chain, I let the stone dangle so it catches the candlelight. Then I speak an invocation, using my magical name.

"I am Fighting Eagle, initiate of the Circle of Harmony. By the agency of this stone, by the power of true magic, I seek the truth about this spirit that has come to disturb me. Let the truth now be revealed."

For a time I stare into the topaz, watching the gold light move and sparkle. Eventually, the air dims and a vision appears.

I move through the sky like a bird, soaring over a coastline, high above the ocean and sandy dunes. Passing the crest of a hill, I gaze down at a crowded scene. Sailing ships, of the kind used hundreds of years ago, lie at anchor. On the beach, men in armor are stalking through a crowd. Dozens of other men lie or kneel in the sand with their hands tied.

The vision drifts closer. The soldiers wear helmets and breastplates like I've seen in pictures of the Spanish conquistadors. As I watch, trumpets blast. Then, to my horror, the soldiers start killing the prisoners, stabbing them with swords and pikes. The men scream and writhe and bleed on the sand as they die.

As the murdering continues, I swoop toward the ground. Gasping, I float among the dying, suffocating in their terror and pain. Then, I look up and see the demon, looming over me. He watches the slaughter with joy.

Slaughter. I remember now. I read about the history of St. Augustine when I first decided to come here. At the time the city was founded, the Spanish and French were fighting over Florida. The Spanish army marched south from their camp at what would later become St. Augustine. They captured more than a hundred Frenchmen who had been shipwrecked. This was also a time of religious wars in Europe. The Spanish were Catholic and these particular French were Protestants. The shipwrecked prisoners were given the choice of converting or being slaughtered. That's where the Matanzas River got its name: the Spanish word for "slaughter."

"You see, I have been here a long time."

I leap out of the chair and whirl. The demon's in the room, hovering a foot in front of me —way too close for comfort. His red eyes stare, and his lips spread in a gruesome smile.

Gasping, I reach behind me, fingers groping on the tabletop. I grab my wand and dagger and hold them crossed in front of the demon's face.

When encountering unfamiliar spirits, I have been taught to first claim my power, then demand the spirit's identity. "I am Fighting Eagle, adept of the Circle of Harmony. What is your true name, spirit?"

The demon touches a long claw to its lips. "Oh, that is very interesting."

"I compel you to tell me your true name!"

It leans back. "I have no objection, young woman magician. I am Alyas. And, as I said, I have been here a long time."

His hand sweeps to the side, pointing a crooked finger. I shift my eyes and see more images, one fading to another, like dreams. They are scenes from different moments of history. A hospital ward with nurses in long gowns and children on narrow beds, shivering with fever. A line of Black men, barefoot and chained, led by a man on horseback. Two men struggling in a dirty barroom, one about to stab the other with a broken bottle. In all the scenes, people groan in pain or cry out in fear. In all the scenes, the demon floats close by, watching with eyes bright and eager.

"Yes, you see? I have often visited the people here. Sometimes I have been invited, sometimes I invited myself. I always enjoy my encounters with mortals."

"What brings you here? Where do you come from?"

"Ah, a wise question ... "

Tightening my grip on the wand and dagger, "I compel you to answer!"

"Very well. I am summoned by the drives and urges of your kind. These coalescence in the outer realms and eventually a creature such as I takes shape. I feed on the mental energy of mortals: anger, fear, hate. But most delicious to me is despair. All things fail in the end. But alone of animals, your kind is gifted with forethought. All mortals know they will sooner or later fail, sooner or later die. It is those moments of despair that I most relish."

A demon that feeds on despair. I shake my head. I think I've compelled him to tell the truth. In any case, I won't get any more from him now. Besides, he's creeping me out.

"Well, Alyas. You're not welcome here with me. So go away now, please."

The demon smiles, glancing with interest at my magical tools. "You *are* a different kind, I must say. I will leave now, as you wish. But we shall meet again, I am certain."

He fades into empty air.

The room is still again in the flickering candlelight.

〜〜〜

Psychic visions can be uncertain and confusing. In the Circle of Harmony, we're taught to test all impressions first by analyzing with the head, then by listening with the heart.

Sitting down again, gazing at my magical tools on the table, I focus on analyzing and listening. Yes, I believe the seeing stone has shown me the truth. This monster has haunted St. Augustine since its earliest history, inciting and taking joy in murder, fear, agony. I believe that he really is a demon, and Alyas is his true name.

All of this is progress.

I've sent him away for now. (Yes, pretty sure I can call it "him.") Also pretty sure he will not leave me alone for long. I'm going to need to raise some serious power if I'm to banish this demon for good.

This will take study, and right now I'm exhausted.

First thing is to get some food. My efficiency apartment has a kitchenette on one wall. I meant to grocery shop over the weekend, but with Ariel visiting I let it slide. Opening the fridge, I confirm there's not much on hand. I settle for a grilled cheese sandwich and a pot of tea.

After getting this fixed, I carry it back to the table and boot up my tablet. Thanks to help from Violet and my friend Molly, who is archiving all this stuff, I have hundreds of pages of Circle of Harmony writings stored on my device. None of it is indexed, though, so I have to do lots of browsing and searching.

The Circle of Harmony was founded in the eighteen-nineties and flourished through the middle of the last century. People from all over came to Harmony Springs to study true magic. Lots of them wrote of their experiences: diaries, treatises on magical theory, records of psychic experiences. As I munch dinner, I search in particular for spells or "formulations" for banishing demons. Some of the possibilities have rather odd titles: *A Formula for Driving Hellish Creatures from Your Sanctum, Dispelling the Vapors of Malevolent Shades, Casting Out Goblins.*"

Any one of these might work for my purposes. I have to read them in detail before I can decide.

While I'm sipping the last of my tea and pondering a paper called "A Record of Shedding a Bothersome Imp," my phone buzzes.

From the ringtone I know it's my mother calling. I'd rather not talk with her just now, but if I don't answer she'll worry.

"Hi, Mom."

"Abby! How are you doing? How's the internship going?"

"Fine. Really well." We chat a bit about the office, the team, and the kinds of work I'm doing.

"And the apartment's still okay?"

My eyes scan the room, looking for bothersome spirits and finding none. "Sure."

Mom knows nothing about my magical self. I've always been careful to keep it that way. Because, she would absolutely not understand, would be convinced I had lost my mind. While Grandma is herself pretty psychic, Mom is the exact opposite—firmly rooted in the physical world.

"Not too hot? Air conditioning's still good?"

"Very cool. How are you, Mom?"

My mother is a high-achiever and something of a workaholic. But since she got promoted to VP and came back from London, her workload actually seems a little lighter. Still, she works excessive hours and commutes into Manhattan from New Jersey.

She tells me a bit about her office and her husband, Jim, my stepdad. But very soon she turns the conversation back to me.

"Have you thought any more about law school applications?"

"Actually, Mom, I haven't. Just working for Sheldon and Bond and getting used to St. Augustine has kept me pretty busy."

"I know, hon. But you really need to research your choices."

Since she's gotten slightly less busy with her job, Mom has taken to micromanaging my plans. Back in January, she sent me a link to a site with a recommended checklist for getting into law school. The list was actually helpful (and mostly jibed with my own research). Following the recommendations, I took the LSATs in April of my junior year. This gives you the opportunity to take them again if you don't score well. My scores were good though, 94%, and added to my summer internship, I'm expecting my law school applications to be solid.

"I'd really like you to consider Pace University in White Plains," Mom is saying. "Very highly regarded for environmental law. Also, NYU is an option."

We've also talked about this before. I've lived in Florida since I started college. Now that she's back in the U.S., Mom really wants me to do law school in or near New York City. And she has a case: Pace and NYU are both excellent schools. But I'm also thinking about University of Miami and UF in Gainesville. Those would let me stay in Florida and be closer to Grandma.

Sigh. "Just give me a little more time to settle in here, okay Mom? Then I promise I'll get back to researching and will seriously consider all the schools."

"Don't wait too long," Mom says. "And keep me informed, all right?"

"Yes. I promise."

We end the call a bit later. Mom says I sound tired so she'll let me go. I put down the phone and stare into space.

My mother can be so intense! I mean, I love her dearly, and she's done so much for me—raised me on her own since I was four when my father died, stood by me through my bizarre, psychically-turbulent adolescence, supported me living in Florida, paid for my college.

But hiding the whole magical side of myself can be exhausting.

And right now I've got a demon to banish.

5. With force beyond all fear and doubt, I vanquish you and cast you out

It's almost midnight by the time I'm ready to perform the banishing. After examining over a dozen magical documents, I settled on one called *A Formula to Forcefully Expel Evil Entities*. It was composed by Peterson Summers, one of the founders of the Circle and purportedly a wise and powerful magician. The ritual is brief but feels very strong. The fact that I know Alyas' name will help in both summoning and banishing him.

At least, that's the theory.

After reading it through three time and memorizing the verses, I take a shower and put on comfortable clothes. I fortify myself with cheese and an apple, and drink coffee to keep alert. I light a candle and place it on the floor in the center of the apartment. With my wand, I trace a circle around the room, visualizing it as a ring of blue fire and stopping at each wall to draw a five-pointed star. Next, I use the dagger to retrace the circle, binding it with mental force.

Standing above the candle, I spread my arms, wand in one hand and dagger in the other, and take ten long, slow breaths.

"I am Fighting Eagle, initiate of the Circle of Harmony. By this wand and the magic of the Springs, I call upon our Friends of Elemental Fire to witness this rite and lend power to my intent."

My mind rises into trance, into attunement with the spirit realms. By the candlelight I see that the circle has grown into a protective sphere, the ring of blue fire and pentagrams still blazing along the edge. Just beyond the sphere, I glimpse shimmering veils of yellow light. I smile, recognizing the salamanders, the Elementals of Fire.

I lift the dagger. "By this blade and the magic of the Springs, I call upon the Elementals of Earth and ask the aid of your strength and power."

Below the burning circle, dim shapes grow from the shadows, like boulders or tree trunks but with eyes and solemn faces.

"Welcome to our Friends of Fire and of Earth. The circle is cast."

Time to get down to business.

I thrust out my arms and speak in my strongest voice. "Now, to this protected circle I summon the spirit Alyas, you who have shown yourself to me in waking and in dream. I summon you by the highest magic. You cannot resist my call."

> By the magic of the Springs
> By the moon beneath her wings
> By the One Who Shapes All Things
> I summon you, Alyas!

On the third repetition, the demon appears through a curtain of light. He stops at the edge of the circle, his eyes taking in the scene— the ring of blue fire, the Elementals, me standing with dagger and wand. His lips part and, for the first time, he seems uncertain.

But he's not alone. A man steps through the same curtain, bearded, heavy-set. It takes me a moment to recognize him: the wizard from my dream atop the lighthouse. No magic robe this time: he's dressed in a sweaty tank-top, shorts, and thick, plastic-rimmed glasses. And he's holding something in his hand—a VR headset?

Well, this is different.

His appearance has distracted me. But then Alyas speaks.

"So you have summoned me, young woman who calls herself Fighting Eagle. Intriguing, I must say." His giant clawed hand touches and presses the sphere of blue light—probing for weakness.

"Yes, I have summoned you to banish you, Alyas. I have the power of true magic and know your true name."

Putting all the calm certainty I can raise into my voice, I recite the chant:

> With force beyond all fear and doubt
> I vanquish you and cast you out.
>
> Nor can you attempt return,
> Lest by this magic you shall burn.
>
> By the power of the Springs,
> By the One Who Shapes All Things,
> I cast you out. I cast you out!

As I speak, I gesture with the wand and dagger and feel the magic flowing from them.

The power jolts Alyas. He looks startled, then angry. The air around him sparks and ripples. Snarling, he shoves hard at the barrier. Behind him, the spirit of the sorcerer watches, fascinated— and maybe afraid. He lifts the VR headset to his eyes, then lowers it again.

Snarls turn to roars. Alyas thrashes and punches at the barrier. Behind him, lightning bolts sizzle and thunder roars. Doing my best to ignore his tantrum, I keep up the chant, summoning and directing the banishing magic.

Finally, the demon's own rage seems to turn back on him. Lighting strikes his head and arms. His body shudders and breaks apart. An explosion of yellow light rips though the room.

Next moment, the demon and his bearded friend are gone.

I wait a few minutes, the candle burning quietly by my feet. Except for a lingering stink of smoke, everything seems normal. Of course, tuning my vision back to the spirit realm, I still see the blue sphere and my Friends of the Elements.

Satisfied that the demon is gone, I thank the Elementals for their help and dismiss them. Following the formula, I carefully unwind and close the circle.

〰〰

I sleep peacefully that night—mentally and physically exhausted. No dreams of demons or anything else that I remember.

But in the morning ...

I check my phone and find a text. Reading it, I almost spit out my coffee.

"I saw what you did to the demon. We have to talk." The text is followed by a link.

Fingers on my lips, staring at the screen, I try to decide what to do.

Then the phone buzzes. Incoming call—the same number as the text.

I swipe my finger and answer. "Who is this?"

"If you tap that link I sent, you'll see me."

Scowling, I open the text, touch the link. It launches a video chat window. I stare at a bearded man with black, plastic-rimmed glasses. I recognize him at once—the demon's wizard friend.

"How did you get my number?"

He grins. "Good question. How did you learn to banish like that?"

I lean back from the screen. "That's a long story. But you haven't answered my question. How did you get my number, and what do you want?"

"Okay. How did we get your number? A little magic, a little hacking. Alyas is good at the one, and I'm really good at the other. What do we want from you? To learn, specifically about your magic. So how did you learn to banish like that?"

"Sorry. That's none of your business. I suggest you leave me alone."

I'm about to disconnect when he says: "Well, that's not gonna happen. Your banishing spell drove Alyas away—for now. But he'll be studying you from afar. You're just too interesting a subject for him to leave alone."

I glare at the screen. "Just what's your connection with the demon?"

He smiles, like he's flattered I should ask. "Well, you could say we're like, business partners."

"What!? What does that mean?"

"Yeah, we're partnering on a project. Are you a gamer by any chance?"

I can't even. This guy is nuts. Not to mention creepy.

This time I do disconnect, without giving him any warning. Then I block his number. If he's an ace hacker, like he claims, the number he called from was probably masked. So he'll probably be able to reach me again with no trouble.

〜〜

So great. Now I not only have a powerful demon who is apparently still stalking me, but a creepy middle-aged gamer hacker guy. Who, might also be a sorcerer capable of summoning a powerful demon.

Yuck.

I need to calm down. I'd like to go for a run or at least do the Daily Ablution. But there's no time for any of that or I'll be late for work. I just have time for a quick shower, a cup of yogurt for breakfast, then on with my clothes and down to the car.

Fortunately, nothing supernatural happens at the office that day. But I do keep checking for apparitions and creepy shadows, and that leaves me frazzled. Gloria and later Nancy ask if I'm doing all right. I tell them, "Of course," and bear down on my tasks.

When I get home, I lock the door. After obsessively inspecting the apartment, I collapse on the sofa. I think about trying the Ablution ritual. Instead, on impulse, I phone Grandma.

She's at home, just starting to cook dinner. After a little small talk, and verifying that she's sitting down, I pour out my troubles. I give her the whole story, from my first sightings of the demon on the bridge and the waterfront, to my dreams, then glimpsing him in the law office, to the banishing formula last night, and then my contact with the hacker guy this morning.

"Abby, I'm so sorry," Grandma says. "This is terrifying."

"Well, nerve-wracking, at least."

"I don't suppose you can call the police about this hacker person?"

"No. I don't know who he is. And he hasn't really threatened me— I mean, physically. He just said they'd be studying me from afar."

"That sounds like stalking to me," Grandma points out. "But I guess you're right. Even if you knew who he was, you can't exactly expect the police to handle a stalking-demon issue."

Right. But thinking about it, I realize this is part of why I'm so upset. The thought of a creepy stalker in the "real world" adds a dimension of vulnerability I haven't quite felt before.

"You can always come home," Grandma says.

Give up? I admit, the thought has occurred to me. Maybe the fear is hitting me so hard because I'm out here alone, trying to live on my own for the first time ever. The past four years I lived with Grandma, and before that with Mom. Maybe this vulnerability feels so vicious because I'm lonely. But then ...

"I can't just quit, Grandma. I have a job here. It's important for my future."

This touches on the whole reason I decided to become a lawyer. That first summer, when I returned to Harmony Springs, I saw again how beautiful it was—and how fragile. All the wild places in Florida are under constant threat, from overdevelopment, from pollution. As a specialist in environmental law, I could do something about that.

I hear Grandma sigh. "I understand your goals, Abby. And I think they're wonderful. But you're still so young. Quitting one internship would not be the end of the world."

I know she's right about that. And somehow, the idea that I could just drop it and move back home is comforting. From the time I was little girl, Grandma has always been a source of comfort and strength.

But no. I'm not a quitter. I've dealt with monsters before. And misguided magicians too. I'm not going to let Alyas and his sorry hacker friend drive me out of town.

"I know you're right about that Grandma. But I'm going to stick it out, at least for now."

Grandma chuckles. "I figured you would. Just remember that you have the option."

"I know. I can't tell you how much that means to me—that I could go home and be with you. You've made me feel better just talking."

"Well, I hope I can do more than that. I'll get with Violet and Kevin, and we'll cast some protective energy around you."

"Is Violet up to that?"

"Kevin said she's doing better. Anyway, they'll both want to know how you're doing." Kevin is Violet's husband—or rather, domestic partner—a retired anthropology professor and also a true magician. He owns a bookstore adjacent to Grandma's antique shop.

"Maybe we can get Molly in on it too," Grandma adds. "Lend us some of that youthful energy."

"Have you seen Molly? I've only had a couple of texts from her since she got back to town."

Molly Quick is my best friend. We met four years ago, my second day in Harmony Springs. She's proven indispensable on more than one of my supernatural capers.

"I haven't seen her myself, but Kevin has," Grandma says. "She's been visiting their house since she got back from school, working on that book about the history of the Circle."

Molly's studying journalism at FSU. She was hoping to land an internship herself, at a Jacksonville TV station. But it fell through at the last minute. She's started a couple of different book projects on magic and the Circle of Harmony.

"Say hello for me, if you see her, Grandma. And to Violet and Kevin too."

After the phone call, I feel much better. Taking a cue from what Grandma said, I work a formula to cast protection around myself and the apartment—and resolve to repeat that every night going forward. Since my banishing formula succeeded in casting the demon out, it makes sense that reinforcing the energy should keep him away.

Plus, it feels good to invoke my power.

That night I sleep soundly, and wake up in time to take a run in the morning. That makes me feel even calmer. Things at the office go fine that day.

Then, in the middle of the afternoon, I get a text from Molly. She arranges to phone me at eight.

"Abby!" Her voice comes bright and chipper over the phone. "How are you doing?"

I'm stretched out on the couch, relaxing. "Better, now that I'm hearing your voice."

"Great! Your grandmother said you were having some evil-entity issues. You always attract the weirdest dilemmas."

"Story of my life, as you well know."

"Yes. You've certainly made my life a lot more interesting. Tell me *all* about it."

As I fill in the details, Molly responds with "oohs" and "ahhs" and asks clarifying questions at many points. When I get to the part about the hacker guy, the "oohs" turn to "ewws."

"Well, I'm not surprised that he masked his phone number," Molly says. "There are apps out there that make that easy. How he tracked down *your* number is another question."

"He did say there was magic involved."

"Right ... But you're doing magic to shield yourself?"

"Yes. I'm going to do that every night."

"Good. And, on that subject, Violet and Kevin and your grandma are going to do a Circle of Harmony ritual on Saturday to help protect you. I'll be joining them."

At first, Molly was hesitant to initiate into the Circle. But she finally took the step after she herself was haunted by a ghost. That was two and a half years ago. Since then, her participation on the magical path has been kind of on and off—even more inconsistent than mine.

"That sounds great, Molly. I really appreciate it."

"They think it might be more effective if you were there. Any chance you could make the trip?"

I hadn't thought of that. Which I do now, for just a moment. "You know, I'd love to. But it's like a two-and-a-half hour drive to Harmony Springs. And I'm going to have weekend work to do for the law office."

"Yeah, I was afraid you'd say that. Okay, we'll go with Plan B. I'll send you a meeting link and you can participate virtually. How's that?"

"*That* sounds awesome."

~~

Saturday afternoon, just before two, I log in to the virtual meeting. Sitting at my work table, gazing at my tablet screen, I'm greeted by Molly's grinning face. In the background I see Violet's narrow living room, with sunlight shining behind the closed window blinds.

"I've got her!" Molly gestures excitedly.

Grandma and then Kevin and Violet walk over and peer into the camera. Kevin is a slim Black man in his late sixties. Violet's in her seventies, with a round face that always looks flushed. Although she's been sick lately, at least on the screen she looks good—bright and eager.

All of them smile and wave, saying how happy they are to see me.

"I believe we are ready on this end," Violet says. "So, if you're ready Abby, we will begin."

"Yes," I answer. "What do I need to do?"

"Just follow along mentally, dear. As best you can, imagine that you are here with us."

She steps back from the camera. Molly shifts her device to give me a wider view. The four of them step to the center of the room and form a circle. Violet, Kevin, and Grandma are wearing ceremonial robes. Molly's in shorts and a T-shirt, but barefoot.

Violet's sleeves hang loose as she spreads her arms. With her wand she spins a circle in the air three times.

"Power of the Springs. Power of the Springs. Power of the Springs."

All of us join her in the chant. Across the virtual connection, I attune myself to the magic of the rite. The power flowing from her wand appears as blue light in my vision.

All is quiet for a moment, then Violet says: "The circle is duly scribed. The perimeter is magically guarded. Only initiates stand within. Therefore, in the name of the spirit Lebab, and the names of our greatly-honored Founders, I declare that the Circle of Harmony is established in this place and time."

Her voice, shaky at first, has grown calm and strong. "Now, dear companions, let us walk to the Springs, the Springs that are Fountains and the Fountains that are way-markers on the path of true magic. Let us review their lessons, that we may be nourished and renewed."

The way stations have been set up along the walls—five paintings representing the five Springs, each with a candle and ceremonial cup. Violet leads the group to the first station, where the portrait shows a white fountain with a single spout of water.

"Before us flows the Fountain of Love—love of knowledge and of truth, which first inspires the magical quest." Violet picks up a clear goblet. "We drink from this Spring to dispel confusion of spirit and see past the illusions of surface appearance."

After taking a sip, she passes the cup to the others. When it's returned to her, she holds it up toward the camera on the other side of the room. "We also share this ritual cup with our dear Fighting Eagle, over there on the computer and in St. Augustine." She takes another sip.

Putting the goblet down, she leads the group to the next station. From my angle, I can't see the painting this time. But Molly is inspired. She hurries over, picks up her tablet and carries it back, holding the camera so I can clearly see the portrait of Endurance.

The ritual continues, moving from Endurance to Balance to the Fountain of Amity. With each stop, my mental connection grows stronger. I reflect with regret about how I have let myself drift away from the path of true magic. Just like with running, I've let my conditioning lapse.

But now circumstances are drawing me back, and I'm glad. I need this energy in my life.

After journeying to each of the five Springs, the group gathers again at the center. Kevin and Molly fetch chairs from the kitchen. They arrange these in a circle, with a fifth chair on which Molly places the virtual me.

When the others are seated, Violet says: "Now, my dear magicians, let us envision a current of light, the clear blue spiritual light of the Springs. This current moves around our circle including also Fighting Eagle, flowing from heart to heart."

Staring at my screen, I picture the blue light and feel it pulsing through my chest.

"Now," Violet says, "as the magical current grows stronger and stronger, let us form our intention. That is, to cast a sphere of protection around our dear friend Abby, known to this circle as Fighting Eagle. Let all the power of the Circle of Harmony, all the magic of the Springs, flow into this sphere, forming a barrier that no evil may penetrate."

Now they draw circles in the air, Violet, Kevin, and Grandma with their wands, Molly moving her finger. In a state of trance now, I feel the power flowing around me, building and brightening, moving forward through space and time to enfold and protect me.

Finally, back in Harmony Springs, Violet raises both arms and shouts. "As we cast, so let it be!"

$$\approx$$

With the ritual ended, the magicians rise and collect themselves. Grandma bends into the camera and checks on how I'm doing. Violet and Kevin also say parting words. They urge me to take care of myself and stay in touch. Finally, Molly carries her tablet back to the table in the corner.

"How was that, Abby?" She's grinning, eyes lit with energy.

"Whoosh. Molly, that was tremendous. Thank you so much for setting it up."

"My pleasure. And ... I've got something else for you. I know you're working some on the weekends, but I insist you take next Saturday off, all day, so we can visit. I will come to you—Okay?"

"Umm, Yeah. I can certainly take one day off. You're sure you don't mind the drive?"

"Not at all. In fact, I've got something planned—something special. Can I spend Saturday night at your place?"

"Of course. I've got a bed and a couch."

"Couch will suit me fine."

"What do you have planned, Molly?"

"I think I'll leave that for a surprise. It will be interesting. And magical. You'll love it, I promise!"

6. At the farmers market and witches festival

"My week was really good. Interesting stuff at work. I'm starting to get the hang of the internship."

"No more demons or creepy gamer hackers?" Molly asks, driving with one hand on the wheel. She's dressed in cutoff shorts and a green T-shirt, which goes well with her frizzy red hair.

"Not a bit. That magic you guys did for me really helped. I'm feeling a lot more grounded. Of course, I'm also keeping up with my own protections."

We're in the front seat of Molly's Corolla as she navigates the narrow streets of St. Augustine. It's 10:30 Saturday morning, a week since our virtual ceremony. Molly's just picked me up at my apartment and now the GPS is guiding her across the northern part of town.

"So, are you going to tell me where we're going?"

She glances at me with a sly grin. "I guess I can reveal the secret— now that I have you in the car."

"Yes ... ?"

"Jacksonville! We'll take Route 1 instead of the Interstate. It's more scenic."

Jacksonville is a little less than an hour's drive. But I have to wonder: "What's in Jacksonville?"

"Well," Molly says, "you know, when I thought I was going to get the internship there, I researched interesting facts about the city.

They have this big farmers market every Saturday, in this really cool location on the water, *underneath* the Fuller Warren Bridge, which is where I-95 crosses the river. So you've got this huge bridge span overhead, and the St. Johns River on the side. Anyway, they combine the farmers markets with different events, and *this* weekend it's a psychic fair and witches festival."

"Oh ..."

"I thought it would be fun: see new sights. And we might pick up some interesting facts—about demons, magic, who knows?"

You have to love Molly's enthusiasm. If I've made her life more interesting, she's certainly made mine more fun.

"Well, in any case, it is great to see you, Molly."

"Likewise, Abby. If nothing else, we'll have a nice lunch."

"And maybe buy some produce."

"Huh?"

"Farmers market, right?"

"Right!"

She turns onto US Highway 1, which runs along the western edge of St. Augustine. There's a river inlet to our left, which you can sometimes glimpse behind the gas stations, shops, and fast-food restaurants. But pretty soon the buildings give way to more open country—fields and wetlands lined with palms and patches of scrub pine, along with an occasional gated community.

Molly tells me about her first year at FSU. Initially, living away from home for the first time, she did some heavy partying. But soon she got bored with that and focused more on her studies—leaving partying "for Saturdays only", as she puts it. Enthusiastic about the prospect of a summer internship in Jacksonville, she felt deflated when it fell through. But she quickly readjusted to spending the summer in Harmony Springs and picked up her old job at the coffee shop. Needing something to occupy her free time, she resumed work on a project she's started and stopped several times in the past—a book about the occult history of the town and the Circle of Harmony.

"How is that going?" I ask her.

"Kind of frustrating," Molly admits. "You know, I started out wanting to write the history of the Circle of Harmony, without going too much into the actual magic. Because, of course, that's supposed to remain secret to all but the initiated. But then, after I initiated, I got more and more interested in the accounts people left behind of their magic activities. So I keep struggling to find the right balance."

"What does Violet think?"

Molly throws up a hand. "She's all over the place about it! She'll encourage me to include stuff about the ceremonies or someone's magical writing. Then she'll read what I've outlined and decide it really ought not to be disclosed."

"Well, that makes it tougher." Violet didn't used to be so indecisive. Privately, I wonder if age and ill health might be catching up with her at last.

Molly may have sensed what I was thinking. "She has been sick a lot lately. I get the feeling she's thinking about her mortality, you know?"

"Yes."

"She doesn't want all the magical knowledge of the Circle to disappear. But at the same time, she doesn't feel comfortable publishing a lot of it."

"What does Kevin say?"

"Oh, he refuses to get into it. He says he owes it to Violet to let her decide."

"So that leaves you kind of stuck."

"Yeah ... But I'll keep working with Violet, as long as she's willing. Because I love her, and she is a really interesting person."

I just nod.

Molly's quiet for a while. When she stops at a red light, she turns to me. "Speaking of magic and book projects: Now that I'm off school and have free time, and my work with Violet keeps stalling, I've got another thought. Remember that book *we* were planning to write together, about sigil magic ... ?"

"Yes, I do."

Sigils are magical diagrams, used to invoke spirits or other powers. Our interest in that form of magic started three summers ago. At the time, I was haunted by the ghost of a Nazi magician and his freaky frog monster—a thought-form born from an Internet meme. That experience led us to Lock Tower in central Florida, where we uncovered sigils developed long ago to invoke Inanna, the ancient goddess.

Now I'm reminded that I saw Inanna recently in a vision. She seemed remote and did not speak, and I wondered if I was to blame, for letting my relationship with her lapse.

I look hard into Molly's eyes. "Do you think we should start studying sigils again?"

She grins. "I will if you will!"

The light turns green and she steps on the gas.

〰〰

As Molly predicted, the site of the farmers market is pretty amazing. Booths and tents stretch for a long way under the span of the I-95 bridge. After parking on a side street, we wander past booths and stalls selling every kind of food imaginable—not just fruits and veggies, but coffee and donuts, bagels and baguettes, meats and seafood packed on bins full of ice. We also pass booths selling arts and crafts, old books, bric-a-brac. Along the way are areas with benches and picnic tables. There's even a small stage where a guy is singing and playing guitar, his performance mixing with the babble of the crowds and the drone of cars and trucks rolling on the highway forty feet overhead.

The Psychic Fair and Witches Festival is set up at the far end of the market, beside the river. Here the vibe's more exotic. Merchandise includes candles, jewelry, tapestries, and incense burners. Booths and tents advertise readings—intuitive, tarot, crystal ball—as well as Reiki and chair massage. Down the hill, at the edge of the water, a drum circle is in progress with people dancing.

Walking in that direction, I notice a woman watching us. She's small, middle-aged, dressed in a long colorful dress and head scarf. She's leaning on a counter in front of a tent. The sign says: "Margaret Greene's Predictions: I will read your future."

Noticing her, Molly stops. "Let's try that one."

"You mean for a reading?"

"Sure. Why not?"

I think about it and shrug. "Not for me. You can if you want."

"C'mon Abby. Lighten up."

We walk over, and the woman smiles a greeting. "Hello, ladies. I'm Margaret. What can I do for you today?"

"How much for a reading?" Molly asks.

"Twenty for tarot cards, ten for crystal ball. The tarot is more detailed, of course."

"I've never done crystal ball," Molly says. "I think I'll try that."

"Sure." Smiling, Margaret glances at me. "And how about you?"

She seems nice enough, but for some reason the idea of a reading doesn't appeal. "I'll just wait here."

"As you wish." She gestures for Molly to step behind the counter. Opening the tent flap, she calls out. "Customer, girls. Would you tend the booth please?"

She holds the flap open and a young woman appears—tall and slim with long blond hair. She steps out, and a little girl follows her, brown-haired, around 10 or 11, with wide, serious eyes. But it's the older girl who seizes my attention. She locks eyes with me and a jolt passes between us. Do I know her? She quickly lowers her eyes as she steps to the counter. The little girl follows, staring at me somberly.

Molly and Margaret Greene have disappeared into the tent.

"Are you having a reading too?" the blond girl asks me, then drops her eyes again.

"Oh, I don't think so. Just waiting for my friend."

"Well, we have some cards and talismans you might like." She gestures at the merchandise set out on the counter top.

I peer at her hard. I'm not sure but ...

"Do you two know each other?" the little girl asks.

The blond girl looks embarrassed.

"I don't think we've met," I say to her. "But you do look familiar. My name is Abby Renshaw."

"Cary Greene."

"Do you live in Jacksonville?" I ask.

"St. Augustine."

It *is* her. Now I'm sure of it: the girl I saw at the waterfront with the demon, and later at the restaurant.

"Maybe that's where I saw you. At that restaurant, *Barnacles*?"

She gives a thin smile. "I tend bar there."

She seems reluctant to talk about it. But I press on. "Yeah, I was there on Memorial Day."

Silence.

I can understand her reluctance, but I have to find out what she knows. "As a matter of fact, I might have seen you earlier that same day, along the waterfront ... "

She shrugs and looks away again. The little girl watches intently. I decide to kick down the door.

"If I'm not mistaken, I saw you with a pelican."

She gives in. "Yes, I remember you now: the sweaty girl across the street."

"Right, I had just run the 5K."

"That explains it ... " She looks down at the counter, wanting to end the conversation.

But I'm not having that now. "Do you remember anyone else there?"

Frowning. "Like ... ?"

"Like a demon?"

Now she's scared. "Did you see it too?"

"'Fraid so."

"She saw it too! I knew it!" That from the little girl, who's staring at me wide-eyed.

"This is my little sister," Cary says. "We call her Hummingbird."

"Oh, that's cute. Nice to meet you."

"Hummingbird is my name," she says, and points to her big sister. "And her name is really Canary."

"Never mind that now," Cary or Canary answers, annoyed.

"What did you make of the demon?" I ask, trying to get back on track.

She lifts a shoulder. "I don't know. Sometimes I see weird stuff like that. Not often. What did you make of it?"

Well, that's a long story. I decide at once it's longer than she wants to hear. "I'm still trying to figure it out."

"Well, it probably means nothing. I haven't seen it again, except a few times in my dreams."

"What happens in your dreams?"

She swallows, reluctant again. "It—Well, it tries to convince me to jump off of—the bridge or the lighthouse or some hotel building ... "

"Wow. I've had that same dream."

"What, it tries to make you jump?"

"No. It tries to make *you* jump. Sorry ..."

Her face squinches up. Then she waves a hand. "It probably means nothing. I've always had weird dreams."

At that moment, Molly and Margaret emerge from inside the tent.

"Very interesting subject," Margaret is saying. "Come back sometime and let me know how it works out."

I take out my phone and say to Cary, "Maybe we should exchange numbers. So we can stay in touch. Just in case ... ?"

Cary considers the offer. "No. Thanks anyway, but I'd just as soon forget the whole thing. I'm pretty sure it's over. And I want to leave it that way."

"Okay. I hope you're right."

"You're sure you wouldn't like a reading?" Margaret asks me.

≈

"What was that all about?" Molly asks me as we're walking away from Margaret's tent. "Exchanging phone numbers?"

"I'll tell you later. First tell me about the reading."

"Not much to say," Molly answers. "The crystal ball looked kind of cool, but I couldn't see anything in it. I asked about sigil magic and how we could best approach it in our book. She said that's a very deep subject. She looked for a while and said she saw many tracks we might take—as if I didn't know that already. Then she said something important could come out of our working on it together, but probably not what I was expecting. Whatever that means."

"Sounds pretty vague."

"Yeah," Molly laughs. "What do you expect for ten bucks? Now what was that about exchanging phone numbers with her daughter ... ?"

I explain that the girl Cary—or Canary—was in fact the girl I saw on the waterfront that day with the demon. I'm about to go into our shared dream when we hear a frantic voice and running footsteps.

"Wait. Wait you two! You have to talk to me!"

Our heads whirl around, then down. It's the little girl, Hummingbird, rushing up the lane toward us. I tell her Hello and introduce her to Molly.

"I must speak with you." She's breathless. "Please."

"Sure."

We walk over to an area with picnic tables and sit down. She looks around anxiously, then begins.

"It's about my sister, Canary. She's a lot more worried than she let you believe. I'm very psychic, and I know."

"She's worried about the demon?"

"Yes. That's why she came up here today, to see my mom and have her do a reading. Mom could see it's real serious, but she didn't say how bad, because she didn't want to scare us. She said she'll do a spell to protect her. But that might not be enough. I'm afraid my sister's in grave danger."

Molly and I exchange a look.

"I'm afraid you may be right," I tell the little girl.

"I know I'm right. I'm very psychic. But I also see that *you* might be able to protect her. Will you do that, Abby, please?"

Not sure how I can protect her—especially if she won't even let me in on what she's going through. But Hummingbird looks so earnest. I finally say, "I'll do my best."

Molly pats her on the wrist. "We both will. We promise."

~~~

"Do you really think she's psychic?" Molly asks. "And what's with the bird names?"

After Hummingbird left, we went over to a stand and bought iced coffees. Now we're back at the same table, with people walking past us, drumbeats drifting up from the waterfront.

"I don't know about the bird names," I answer. "Or how psychic the little girl is. But I do get the feeling her sister's in danger from that demon."

Molly gazes into her iced mocha. "Well, we did promise to protect her."

"We promised to try." I think it over. "I guess I could extend the protections I'm casting every night to include Cary. That seems to be working for me, so far."

"Good idea," Molly says. "Maybe include the rest of her family too?"

I stare down at the bright lawn full of drummers and dancers, and beyond it to the river with boats floating by. The demonic power seems an impossible distance away from this tranquil place.

"Sure, why not? But I don't think the mother and little girl are in danger. I get the feeling this demon is local to St. Augustine."

So that night, Molly and I work together, weaving a circle of protection around ourselves and my apartment, then extending the energy to also shield Cary Greene and her family.

After that work is done, we sit up late drinking tea and going over our collections of sigils. We both have dozens of the magical drawings scanned in on our phones and tablets.

Most came from Circle of Harmony archives. As heir to the Circle's knowledge, Violet kept boxes and boxes of papers stored in her house and garage. Molly has been exploring these writings the past three years, and some of them included sigils. There were also books published, three volumes called "Sigils of the Order." Kevin keeps those in a climate-controlled reading room in the back of his bookshop. Molly and I have both read through some of those at different times.

But the Circle of Harmony was not the only magical order. From early on, other groups and individual occultists worked with sigils. Molly's found sigils used to invoke all kinds of spirits and powers—astrological signs, planets, ancient deities, angels, even demons. Definitely staying away from that last type, we both agree.

Finally, there is my collection of sigils from Lock Tower. Some of those—the Sigils of Inanna—I copied from carvings on the top of the tower. Others I "borrowed" from the library of Emanuel Lock, the man who built the tower. (To be fair, Lock's ghost urged me to make copies of his sigils, and I did return the actual papers.)

"Same old problem," Molly complains, hands in the air. "There's just so much information, I don't know where to begin."

"Well, that is why we've never gotten this project off the ground."

"I know. There are already books and websites out there that examine sigils. So whatever we write has to be unique. And our only unique angle is that we have a lot of unpublished content from the Circle of Harmony. But, then we run into the same issue about what's okay to share and what needs to stay secret." Her mouth clamps with frustration. "And *that's* the same problem I've having with the history of the Circle project."

"I sympathize. I don't know that we need to keep all the magical knowledge secret. But Violet's been around a lot longer than we have. I guess you'll just need to keep working on her about that."

"Oh, I will, I promise you."

We're quiet for a while, scrolling through images of sigils for invoking spirits. They resemble tiny drawings of birds and fish. I think about Cary Greene who seemingly talks to pelicans ...

"Here's a thought," I tell Molly. "Everyone who studies magic is going to have their own take, because magic taps into your inner being. So suppose you and I pick out some sigils that speak to us, and meditate on them—put ourselves in touch with whatever spirit or power they represent, and see what happens. Maybe that could be our unique angle."

Molly touches her chin, ponders the idea. "Well, I'm not great at meditating—as you know, too easily distracted. But I think it's worth a try. If nothing else, it would be good practice for me."

"Okay."

"Yeah, but, we really do need to stay on track this time. With you here and me in Harmony Springs, that's going to be tough."

"What do you suggest?"

"How about we meet online? For an hour or two, at least twice a week. Say Monday's and Thursdays, 7 p.m. What do you think?"

I'm grinning. Visiting with Molly twice a week? Regular meetings to keep me on track with my much-needed magical studies? What's not to like?

7. The crow did say to trust you

Moving down the side aisle of a small church, I keep to the shadows, avoiding squares of colored light on the floor—daylight shining through stained glass. I'm focused on the space in front of the altar. A tall man stands there, gray-haired, dressed in a priest's gown.

But something's wrong.

The "priest" is not facing the altar and praying. He's facing the opposite way, chanting verses that sound like Spanish or Latin. With each chant, he gestures sharply with the silver wand grasped in his hand.

In front of him, on the steps that lead to the altar, a spiral of gray appears. The air hums. The spiral grows and widens as the man's chanting gets louder. With his last flourish of the wand, the light blinks and turns black.

Out of the blackness steps the demon.

The priest and the demon stare at each other. I stand frozen, hoping they won't spot me.

Then a movement appears at the edge of my sight. In the darkness on the side of the altar, another figure—the wizard hacker guy. He's recording the scene on his phone ...

Waking, I stare at the ceiling.

Third time I've dreamed of the demon in the week and half since Molly's visit. Each time is different, but similar. The scenes all come from different times in the past—from the history of St. Augustine,

I'm pretty sure. There's always a single person who calls, or is visited by, the demon. Always, my creepy hacker friend is there to capture the scene.

And always I make the same response—as I do now.

I climb out of bed, fetch my wand and dagger. Standing in the center of the apartment, I draw a banishing pentagram, then mentally cleanse the space.

When that's done, I stand for a few moments, puffing my breath, settling my emotions.

The clock tells me it's only a half-hour till my normal wake-up time. No point in trying to sleep. Instead, I start the coffee maker, check my phone for messages, scan the news. After that, I use the extra time to browse through some magical writings and sigils.

I've done three online meetings with Molly since her visit. Every day, I've studied and meditated on at least one sigil.

This is my life now: banishing magic for protection, research on sigils, lots of work for the law office, running nearly every day to keep fit. Not a bad life at all—apart from the demon dreams.

I'm eating breakfast, cereal and coffee, when my phone buzzes. It's Grandma calling, so I pick it up.

"Hi, Abby. Have you got a minute? I won't keep you long."

"Of course, Grandma. I always have time for you."

She asks how I am and I assure her I'm okay, that the protective magic the group did for me seems to be holding up. This leads me to ask about Violet.

"I haven't seen her. Kevin says she's doing *pretty* well, still trying to recoup her old energy though, so pretty much staying at home."

"Oh ..."

"Yeah. We're all getting older, Abby. That kind of relates to what I wanted to talk to you about. I think I mentioned there might be some changes with the shop. I'm considering taking on a partner. How would you feel about that?"

"Um ... fine. I mean, it's your shop, Grandma. And I can see how your getting some help might be great. Who's the partner?"

"It's a Chinese man, Alan Tsai. Actually he's from Taiwan. He owns two other antique businesses, in Orlando and Ocala. You know Jenny Nesheim is closing her shop next door. Alan wants to take over that space and combine it with my shop. He'd be bringing in a lot more stock, most of it imports."

"Wow."

"I know. Big changes. But he's a very nice man. And he has a lovely daughter, Amelia, who would work here with me. The truth is, Abby, while I don't like to admit it, the shop has gotten to be a lot for me to handle. It would be nice to offload some of the work and responsibility. But I didn't want to make a deal without checking how you feel about it."

How I feel is ... a little stunned. It's not like I envisioned owning the antique shop as part of my future or anything. But I've helped Grandma in the shop on and off the past four years. It's become part of my cozy little home in Harmony Springs—and I hate to see that changing.

But nothing lasts forever.

"I feel fine about it, as long as you do, Grandma."

"Well, mixed feelings. None of us like to let go of the good things. But since you're okay with it, I'll probably go ahead."

♒

"What do you think of this one?" Molly's face asks from the corner of the display.

The main window shows a line drawing, dark red on white. A circle with an arrow pointing out of it at the top right, a triangle in the middle of the circle, a sword and spear standing on either side. The drawing is labeled: "Sigil of Mars."

"Feels powerful," I answer. "Definitely Mars-like."

It's Thursday, a little past 8 p.m., and we've convened for our twice-weekly study session.

"Yeah, it attracts me," Molly says. "More than most of them so far. I've tried meditating on it once and didn't get much, but I think I'll give it another shot."

Truth be told, I'm also struggling to get much from my sigil meditations. Mostly I go into light trance. Feelings come up, but no visions and certainly no profound disclosures. I've tried a number of sigils drawn by early members of the Circle of Harmony, and also a few from other sources. But I keep getting pulled back to the ones that came from Lock Tower. Those sigils, developed by Emanuel Lock and his partner, Kurt Fredrich Gensen, mostly depict Mesopotamian deities and other spirits from mythology, including the Goddess Inanna.

Molly passes control of the screen to me and I show her the ones I've worked with the past few days. One is for Enki, god of wisdom, and another for Utu, called "the all-seeing."

"You know, I've been looking at Mars and some of the other Roman and Greek gods," Molly says. "Maybe that will turn out to be the focus for our book: "*Sigils of Ancient Gods* or something like that ...""

We explore that idea for a while, looking at more of the sigils from the Lock Tower collection. When we're about to sign off the call, Molly brings up something else.

"I've been meaning to ask you, have you heard any more from that girl, Cary Greene?"

"Nope."

"I do hope she's okay. We promised Hummingbird we'd keep an eye on her."

"I know. I'm still sending her the protection every night. And I *have* checked on her a few times with my seeing stone. I haven't seen anything happening, so I'm thinking she's okay."

But, after ending the call, I start to wonder. Just because I've got the demon problem mostly under control, and just because I haven't seen any blatant danger around Cary Greene, can I be sure she isn't in trouble? ... And I *did* promise her little sister that I would do my best to protect the girl.

Sigh.

Next day is Friday. After I get off work, I walk down to the waterfront and stop at *Barnacles*, the restaurant where Cary Greene works. I find her in the upstairs room behind the bar, so I take a seat on one of the stools.

When she spots me, I think I catch a quick frown. But soon she comes over, because she has to. I give her a friendly smile.

"Hi, remember me?"

"Sure. What can I get you?"

"Club soda."

When she brings it, I raise a hand. "I wanted to see how you're doing. You know, with *things* ...?"

She glances around, uncomfortable. "Not the place to talk about that."

"I understand. When can we talk?"

Unhappy face. "Okay. I get off at nine. Meet me outside, and we can have a chat."

"Cool. I'll wait."

It's now 7:45. Since I haven't had dinner, I order a sandwich. When she brings the bill, I put a nice tip on my credit card.

She meets me outside the restaurant just after nine. At her suggestion, we cross the wide avenue and walk toward the water. The Castillo de San Marcos lies to our left, and the Bridge of Lions spans the river a few blocks to the right. An oblong moon rides high in the east. Cool breezes flow in off the water. We take a bench by the seawall. I sit while she stands, facing me and resting one foot on the bench.

"Here we are," she says. "You wanted to chat."

"Yeah. I'm sorry to bother you at work. But I had no other way to reach you. And I *did* promise your little sister I would, well, keep an eye on you."

Her frown becomes a grim smile at the mention of her sister.

"Yes, your sister *Hummingbird*," I continue. "First, I have to ask, is your name really Cary or Canary?"

Her mouth pulls back at the corner. "Legally, it's Canary, I'm sorry to say. My mom is weird. She has three daughters, from three different men. My older sister is Raven, and you've met Hummingbird."

"I actually think that's kind of cute."

"Yeah, well, try living with it."

When I don't answer, her harsh expression softens. "Sorry if I've seemed unfriendly. It's just that, growing up with a psychic witch mother who names her daughters after birds—it's crazy. After a while you get tired of the craziness. That's why I finally left and moved here, to live a normal life."

"Only now the craziness has followed you?"

My insight startles her. "Yeah."

"I understand that. Believe me." Heck, I've often tried to escape, or at least minimize, the weirdness in my own life. Which brings me to the point of our conversation: "Have you seen any more of the demon?"

"Well ..." Guarded answer. "Some. In my dreams."

"Yeah. I've been dreaming about him too."

She peers at me hard, like she's struggling to decide how much to say.

Suddenly she turns her head. A black bird is walking along the sea wall, a grackle or crow. I can just make it out in the moonlight. Canary Greene watches it, and her lips move as if she's whispering. Then the bird hops from the wall and flies toward the bridge.

Canary faces me, looking puzzled.

I'm sort of puzzled myself. "You *do* talk with birds then?"

She shrugs. "Birds. Sometimes dolphins. Dogs and cats, of course. Animals have souls you know. They can tell us a lot. Sometimes I get psychic insights."

Her intense face slips into a laugh. "I know. I told you I'm trying to escape all the crazy stuff, and here I am talking to a crow."

"I've seen crazier. The crow tell you anything useful?"

"Yeah. She said I should trust you."

"Oh, good. I'm flattered."

She can't help but laugh again. But it's a gloomy laugh. "All right, trusting you now. It's actually gotten pretty bad—the demon, I mean. I feel him around me, more and more. Sometimes I glimpse him in the dark. in my bedroom or my bathroom mirror. Sometimes I hear whispers. But I can't quite tell what he's saying."

Her shoulders shake. "Creepy."

"For sure."

I was right to come find her tonight. I definitely need to do something about this. "Listen, Cary. I'll do what I can to help. I would like to exchange phone numbers, so we can keep in touch."

She eyes me, skeptical. "What can you do?"

"Well, no promises. But I have studied different systems of magic, and I've dealt with nasty spirits before."

"So, you're like a demon-hunter?"

I've taken out my phone. "No claims. No promises—except to do my best."

She smiles and reaches to her back pocket for her phone. "Well, the crow did say to trust you."

8. Of course, there's also the normal part

I'm really grateful for this internship. More and more, I'm getting the hang of legal work. And with all the anxiety and uncertainty of the demon-esque parts of my life, it's nice to have something solid and normal.

Like right now. I'm in a staff meeting, dressed in a crisp white blouse and business slacks, diligently typing on a laptop. All this feels like the normality that Cary Greene so desperately wants in her life. I can so relate.

I've gotten good at taking the minutes, to the point where Gloria relies on me to do it. She no longer types her own, just writes notes on a legal pad.

The discussion has moved on to a troublesome client, a woman named Cassandra Lorenzo who recently used our firm to help her buy a house. The property dates to the 1800s and is located in the northern part of the historic district, near the place known as the Old Jail.

It's more common in a real estate transaction for the seller to hire the attorney, but Cassandra wanted her own lawyers involved. I remember attending the closing, my first week here. Cassandra impressed me as an odd character, a middle-aged woman with a tan complexion and intense, serious eyes.

Now it seems she wants to reverse the sale and get her money back. The seller, of course, has refused. Cassandra insists it's impossible for her to live in the house because it's haunted by malevolent spirits.

"Wait a minute," Teresa the senior partner says. "Isn't she the woman who claimed to be a paranormal expert or something? Didn't she specifically *want* that house because it was reportedly haunted?"

"That's the one," Larry the other partner answers. "Her complaint is that all of her research indicated several ghosts were known to haunt the property, but that there is some sort of poltergeist or evil spirit that was never mentioned, that it's destructive and terrifying, and this should have been disclosed by the seller."

The team members look at each other with shrugs and sarcastic smiles. Personally, I don't find the matter so completely bizarre and amusing. But that's just me.

"Even if that's true, she has no case," Teresa says. "Under the law it's not the responsibility of the seller to disclose distressed property." She glances at me and explains for my benefit. "Basically, Abby, that means it's *buyer beware*."

"I tried to tell her all that," Larry says. "But she still insists on meeting with me. She says there must be something we can do, and she is still our client."

"Okay, meet with her then," Teresa agrees. "But for god's sake, don't make any promises."

"Don't worry." Larry turns to me. "She's coming in at three today. Why don't you sit in, Abby? Good experience for you, dealing with a difficult client."

~~~

So, later that day, I carry my laptop into Larry's office to meet with the difficult client. Ms. Lorenzo is a flashy dresser, bright blue and orange dress, silver necklace with multiple ornaments. She carries a white vinyl purse, and her phone in a white case.

"I really need you to do something for me," she explains to Larry. "Of course I expected the house to be haunted. That's *precisely* why I bought it. I've been a paranormal researcher for almost twenty years. As you must know, with its long and varied history, St. Augustine is considered *the* most haunted city in the United States. That is *precisely* why I decided to move my practice here."

"Your practice?" I ask. Since Larry asked me to take notes, I want to make sure I have all the details.

She looks at me with lowered eyebrows, not happy at the interruption. "Uh, yes, Ms. … Renshaw. Along with my research and writing, I am known for paranormal investigations. I also do psychic readings, for an exclusive list of clients."

Satisfied that I've gotten that, she turns back to Larry. "But in all my experience, Mr. Sheldon, I have never—and I mean never—come across anything so malevolent as this creature that haunts my new property. I don't mean the odd evil whisper or crashing footsteps in the night. This thing has literally broken dishes, toppled one of my bookshelves, turned on the stove so it nearly burned down the house. My poor poodle, Gabrielle, was having a nervous breakdown. So now I'm having to pay to board her!"

Fingers touching in front of his face, Larry takes a breath. "I do understand the problem, Ms. Lorenzo. But as I told you on the phone, from the legal point of view there's really nothing we can do. When someone buys real estate in Florida, the onus is entirely on the buyer to investigate the suitability of the property. Basically, you bought the house as is."

The client rolls her eyes. "But I should have been warned about the malevolence of the spiritual occupants!"

Larry just looks at her, helplessly.

"Listen," she says. "I have a large social media following, both blogs and videos. I am what they call an *influencer*. If you won't help me, it seems my only recourse is to publicize this trauma. Which I am quite prepared to do. Now, should my narrative say that my law firm—which I employed in good faith—is assisting me to find a remedy, or that Sheldon and Bond has been utterly unhelpful and *abandoned* me?"

Larry winces at this. I doubt that he thinks she can do the firm much harm. Still, bad publicity is never good.

His fingertips part, hands lifted in a gesture of appeasement. "Tell you what, Ms. Lorenzo. We will look into the matter further. If we can find *anything* in the case law, any precedent that might give us a chance to overturn the sale, we will let you know."

Now she looks suspicious. "What will this cost me?"

"For the research, nothing. If we find a possible case, we'll let you know." He stands up to indicate the meeting is over. "Remember, Sheldon and Bond stands behind our clients."

Cassandra nods, rises from her chair, and thanks him. When she's left and shut the door, Larry collapses into his chair. He heaves a sign and rolls his eyes emphatically.

"I'd like you to take the first pass on this, Abby. See if you can find *anything* in case law where buyer complaints resulted in overturning a sale. Most importantly, document every case you check—no matter how tangential. Just a paragraph or two of summary. You're not likely to find any precedents in our favor, but we need to be able to show the client thorough research."

"Um ... Okay."

What was I saying about this legal internship being the one normal part of my life? Might have to rethink that point.

9. Wasn't that amazing?

Hands gripping the wheel, I watch the road swerving toward me. Reflections of headlights and streetlights shine on the wet pavement. It's raining hard, the windshield wipers beating. Suddenly, the road curves sharply and I twist the wheel. The tires skid.

Going too fast!

I glance down, wanting to ease up on the gas pedal, press the brake.

Not my feet! I see men's business shoes and trousers.

"Faster! Faster!"

The voice hisses beside me. My head jerks and I see the demon, leaning close to me from the passenger seat. The car accelerates.

No!

I try to lift my foot off the gas. Instead, my whole body zooms backward and bumps. Now I'm in the backseat of the SUV. A man is driving, a terrified look on his face. Alyas whispers in his ear.

"Faster. Faster!"

Stop! I try to scream, but I have no voice.

The SUV rushes forward, heading for another bend in the road. Past the curve I see a sidewalk and beyond it, a seawall. The engine's roar mixes with the growl of the demon.

A violent jolt and then we're flying, high over the sidewalk and the wall, arcing down toward the black water.

I wake up, gasping. I jump out of bed and stand, shaking, My hands come up to clutch my heart. It takes a few minutes for my breathing to slow.

I go to find my wand so I can banish the fear. My phone lies on the table and I see a message:

"Wasn't that amazing?!"

~~~

After some extra-strong banishing magic, I shut off the lights and go back to bed. But I'm afraid to even shut my eyes. Not only are the demon dreams getting more frequent, but that one felt really intense and scary.

And obviously, gamer hacker guy was there and saw it all.

And now he's stalking me again in real life.

In the morning, things go way past creepy. As I'm sipping my coffee, I pick up the phone. No new text messages and no emails from the office. I take a minute to check the weather app and then scroll through local news. That stops me cold.

Last night, after 2 a.m., an SUV crashed over the seawall in the historic district and plunged into the Mantanzas River. The driver, a middle aged businessman, was killed. A photo on the news site shows the black vehicle being pulled from the water, the Bridge of Lions standing gray in the distance.

The dream was real. A guy was killed.

My protective magic is not good enough. I have to do something more about this demon.

But what?

If only I could talk to the hacker guy, I might figure something. Of course, he masks his phone number. Then I think of something else. It's a long shot, but nothing to lose. I switch back to my text messages and find the first one he sent me, with the link to the video chat.

By now, the chat has expired. But when I try the link it opens a browser with the expiration message. It's a high-tech gamer site, with menu options that include discussion boards and video chat. The page identifies the member who set up the chat: RJWizard. When I go to his profile page, there's statistics of his different game activities, but no personal info. But there *is* a link to send him a private message. To do that, it turns out, I have join the site. So I set up a profile with the handle "COH" (for Circle of Harmony). That's easy enough. Then I send RJWizard a message.

"I got your text about the SUV crash. We need to talk."

Leaving it there, I get dressed for the office. Before leaving the apartment though, I check the site again. RJWizard has sent me a message with a link.

I don't have much time before work, but this is important.

I open the link. Shortly, RJWizard appears on the screen. He squints at me through his heavy glasses.

"So, you wanted to talk to me. And you figured out a way. Smart, COH girl. Very good."

"I have my moments. What happened last night, with the SUV crashing, you know that was real, right?"

A crooked smile. "Wasn't that amazing? And I recorded it all."

I make my voice slow and flat. "A man was killed."

He waves it off, like it's not important. "I know. People get killed all the time."

"Do you murder people all the time?"

His tone goes defensive. "Hey! I didn't murder anybody. Alyas—"

"You're partnering with Alyas, or so you said."

"Yeah. And he's a demon. When you deal with demons, stuff happens."

"That's your answer?"

He shifts a hand. "Look. Things got out of control, I admit. Alyas got under the guy's skin and ... accelerated a certain drive in his brain—Ha! Get it? *Accelerated. Drive.* I made a double pun there."

I scream at him: "This is not funny!"

"Oh, come on, girl, don't be such a buzz kill. People die. The whole world is going to die. None of it matters. The sooner you realize that, the sooner you'll be free to enjoy yourself."

Keep control, Abby. I need to understand this guy as best I can, so I can look for clues for stopping him. "And what do you enjoy, RJWizard?"

"Ha. Call me Jeremy. What do I enjoy? *Experience*, the more intense the better." He holds up a VR headset. "See? I'm capturing all the things the demon does, recording the scenes as data through a little magic he did for me. The playbacks are incredible, not just sensory, but *emotional*, super intense. That's the project we're collaborating on, making it into a game. It will be the most immersive game ever!"

Okay, to him it's a game. But there's a human being in there somewhere. I have to try to reach him. "Listen, Jeremy. A man died last night. Not in a game, in real life. *A person died.* This has to stop."

"No it doesn't. Alyas is a demon. How are you going to stop him? How are you going to stop me? Even if you could find me, which you can't, how would you make me stop?"

Trying to sound tough: "Don't underestimate me."

"Oh, I don't. Neither does Alyas. That's why he keeps getting in touch with you. I think he wants you in the game."

I'm trying to think of what else to say when Jeremy decides he's had enough. Without warning, he reaches down to the keyboard. "Bye, now! Talk soon!"

The screen blinks and white text appears: "Meeting Ended."

~~~

"God, Abby. That's awful!" Molly's face on the screen shows a grimace. "And you haven't heard from him again?"

We're on our scheduled Thursday call, thirty-six hours since my chat with Jeremy.

"No. I sent a couple of messages, but he ignored them. At least I haven't seen the demon again, or heard of anymore deadly accidents."

Molly sighs. "You better keep pumping up the protective magic, girl."

"Oh, I am. For me and for Canary." I glance to the left part of the screen, where I've displayed another of the Lock Tower sigils. "I haven't made much progress on the sigil study, I'm afraid. Too distracted."

"Well. You've got a lot to distract you!"

"I know but ... I keep feeling drawn to the sigils of Inanna. But meditating on them isn't getting me anywhere. I'm just not able to attune myself the way I used to. Maybe it *is* all the distractions ..."

"Or maybe ..." Molly frowns. "Do you think the demon could be blocking you?"

I hadn't thought of that. "Perhaps ..."

"I mean, I have that problem all the time," Molly goes on. "You know me, too easily distracted. But the fact that you're having the same problem makes me wonder. Maybe the demon doesn't want you working on the sigils. Maybe that's a kind of power he fears."

"Yeah. You may be on to something there." And that thought leads me to another. "There was something Jeremy said, something like: 'the demon accelerated an impulse that was already in the driver's brain.' Maybe that's how he works. Not just taking control of people, but finding something inside them that he can use."

"Interesting," Molly says. "How would that apply to you?"

Good question. "I'm not sure ..." Could Alyas be distracting me because at some level I *want* to be distracted? Does part of me not want to even *do* magic anymore? Live a normal life, like Canary Greene said ... "I'm going to have to think hard about that."

"Right," Molly says. "I'll do some research on demons. See if there's anything about them gaining power over people by using what's already in their minds. Maybe there's a way to counter that."

After we end the call, as I fold down the tablet screen, my eye catches a shadow in the corner. For just a second, I think I spot Alyas, watching me.

∿

The sigils of Inanna are circles with tiny eight-pointed stars evenly spaced around the edge. There are eight of the stars in each sigil, and eight sigils in all. The sigils differ in the lines that are drawn to connect some or all of the pointed stars.

I gaze at a sigil on my tablet screen: brightly colored stars with dark lines. In this case, the lines connect every other star on the circle, forming two perfect squares. This sigil is the *Eye of Inanna*. I've chosen it because I need to invoke clear vision.

For a long time, nothing happens. I keep wanting to give up. But each time that thought surfaces, I take a deep breath and keep looking.

Eventually, the lines and colors blur. I feel my body sinking. At last, I'm moving into a trance ...

I walk through a giant room, stone floor and round columns, paintings glimpsed in torchlight—an enormous, ancient temple. A wide stairway leads me down. It grows darker and darker. I hear voices, faint, whispery. I'm frightened, but I keep moving.

The stairs end and I walk down a long, curving tunnel: plain stone walls in shadowy light. *Why am I here?*

Trying to find the Goddess Inanna, to free her power. In one of the myths, Inanna was trapped in the Underworld, the "Great Below." Spirits were sent to free her.

Sharp pain slices my wrists. Looking down, I see that my hands have disappeared. My feet look far away, and now they too are fading.

I have to get out of here.

But which way is out?

Far ahead, I see a light.

The light swims toward me. I realize I'm back in my apartment, staring at the sigil on the screen.

Well, at least I got a vision this time.

Not that it helped any.

10. Another weird dream?

Midnight over the Bridge of Lions. Overcast. No moon or stars. Near the top of the bridge, a young woman casts a faint shadow. She has climbed over the rail and stands on the narrow strip of concrete, leaning out over empty space and the water far below.

Canary Greene.

Behind her lurks another shadow, huge and bulky with blazing eyes—Alyas.

My body is swept toward him until he is inches away. He bends over and whispers in my ear. "If you don't come here now, I will push her, and she will die."

I jump out of bed, my head swinging back and forth to search the room.

Another weird dream?

No! This is real. This is now. I'm certain of it. The demon is going to push her off the bridge. And it will happen soon, unless I stop it.

No time to think, only act. I pull on jeans, a shirt, running shoes.

Too far to run. I'd be too late. Need to drive. I grab my keys and wallet. And my wand. I'll need that too.

Seconds later, I'm running down the outside stairs.

Minutes later, I'm driving onto the bridge. The road is only two lanes. There'll be no place to park. But I'll have to risk that. Not enough time otherwise. I hate to think about leaving my car on the road. I'm very attached to my little Mazda, have even given her a name, Veronica, because she's such a cool girl. Luckily, this time of night there's hardly any traffic. I only pass one car, going the other way.

At the top of the bridge stand four towers, two on either side of the road. Between them lies the central span. As I approach the first tower, I see Canary Greene on the right.

Just like in my vision, she's climbed over the rail and stands with her back to it, holding on with both hands, looking down at the water.

I don't see the demon, but I know he's there.

I check my rearview. Nothing coming. No other choice but to jam on the brakes.

I leave the motor running and turn on the blinkers. Grabbing the wand, I step out onto the bridge. Canary hasn't looked at me. Should I call her? Last thing I want to do is startle her so she loses her grip.

Quietly, I slip onto the sidewalk. When I've gotten within a few yards of Canary, I see the demon. He's standing right behind her. He could easily reach out a hand to push her over.

But he's staring at me, smiling, amused.

I raise my wand, trace a pentagram and whisper. "Alyas, I have the power of true magic and I banish you from this time and place." Repeating the pentagram, I add the chant I used the first time I banished him.

> With force beyond all fear and doubt
> I vanquish you and cast you out.
>
> By the power of the Springs,
> By the One Who Shapes All Things,
> I cast you out. I cast you out.

The demon's smile widens.

Then he vanishes.

"Eeek!" Canary Greene gasps. "What the hell?"

"It's okay, Cary. Just a little eh … mishap."

She looks at me, amazed, terrified. I hurry over, and she reaches out an arm. I grip her wrist and guide her to climb back over the rail.

~~~

Happy to say that Veronica did not get rear-ended on the Bridge of Lions. After getting a confused Canary into the car, I drive to the other side of the bridge, turn around, and head back to St. Augustine.

Incoherent at first, Canary slowly remembers some of what happened. She left work at *Barnacles* at eleven. Even though she felt extra tired, she followed an impulse and walked along the waterfront. She spotted someone in the distance, near the base of the bridge. At first, she thought it was an old boyfriend.

That's the last thing she remembers.

Luckily, she is coherent enough to direct me to her home. She lives in an apartment house a few blocks north of the historic district—not far, in fact, from the law office where I work.

When I stop the car in front of the building, she turns to me, looking vague and uncertain.

"How about I come in with you? Make sure everything's all right?"

"Yeah. Good idea."

As soon as we cross the threshold I know it was a *really* good idea. I can't actually see the demon, but I can feel his energy permeating the one-room apartment like an evil smell. I shudder.

Canary looks at me, her expression growing more worried.

"You know what?" I hold up my wand. "Why don't you go change or lie down or whatever you want to do. With your permission, I'll do a little protective magic for this place."

"Yeah. Good."

After centering myself and visualizing the Springs of Harmony, I perform the same protective rite I've been using for my own home.

In fact, I perform the rite three times. Only then am I satisfied that the space is cleansed and the barriers strong.

Meantime, Canary has gone into the bathroom and changed into a nightgown. For the last two repetitions of the rite, she's been lying on the single bed, staring at me.

Exhausted now, I collapse into an armchair.

"Wow," she says. "Thanks for that."

"You're welcome."

She sits up on the bed. "Guess I was too dazed to ask before. But how did you happen to find me getting ready to jump off the bridge at midnight?"

"Oh. I saw it in a dream—or vision. I guess because I promised to protect you, I got a psychic warning."

"Ah." She ponders that for a moment. "You know, I'm really glad I listened to that crow who told me to trust you. Can I fix you some tea?"

"Love some."

11. Snapping out of it

I don't get home till almost dawn and immediately fall asleep. Luckily, although it's a Monday, it's the third of July. The law office is closed for a long weekend.

I wake up mid-afternoon. While the coffee's brewing, I check my phone.

Text from an unknown number: "Last night was a test," followed by a link to the gaming site.

I wait till I've fortified myself with coffee and cereal before opening the link. After about a minute, a window opens and Jeremy's wide face appears.

"Hey there, COH Girl. You did well: answered the summons, banished the demon. You passed the test. Now he's really interested in you."

Too tired for this. "What do you want?"

"Not me. I'm just the coder, the gamemaster, if you will. It's about what you want, you and Alyas. You're the contestants, see? By the way, I like your handle, COH—that would be for 'Circle of Harmony', right? Very cool. I'll use that for your handle in the game, unless you'd rather something else ...?"

"Listen, Jeremy. This has gone far enough."

"Oh, don't be like that. Let me show you some of the game before you decide."

His image blinks off and a video appears. The camera's inside an old church, moving down the center aisle. It looks suspiciously like one of my demon dreams. But there is no old priest this time. The altar stands empty.

Until Alyas appears, fading into view in the air above the altar. It's a 3D image, but doesn't move.

"I'm still working on the animation," Jeremy says in voice-over. "But you get the idea."

"Listen to me: I don't want to play your stupid game."

Jeremy's face reappears, unconcerned. "But you *do* want to banish the demon. Keep him from doing more damage, right? This is the way. Alyas has promised not to crash any more cars or make anyone commit suicide as long as you keep him occupied with the game. See? I'm doing a good deed here. Setting it up so you two magical opponents can battle it out in a virtual world, with no harm done in the real world."

This is too weird—even by the standards of my life. Of course, I can't trust anything Jeremy RJWizard Creepy Hacker Guy says. And even if he *is* telling the truth, neither of us can trust Alyas.

On the other hand, I am plainly being called to vanquish this demon, if I can. One thing I've been forced to learn: your duty as a true magician will keep slapping you in the face until you accept it. And, if I agree to play along, it *might* limit Alyas' damage in the real world. And it might also help me learn more about the demon, discover any weaknesses, so I banish him for good.

Still, I make my answer evasive. "I'll have to think it over."

Jeremy grins. "Excellent. We'll be in touch."

He clicks, and my screen goes blank.

〰

"We have a special guest joining our meeting today," Molly announces as soon as our video call opens.

This is our normally scheduled Monday session, but not at the normal time. She texted me an hour ago and asked if we could meet at four instead of eight. I assumed she might have holiday plans for the evening, but as soon as I see her I know that's not it. I recognize the wallpaper in the background: Violet's little kitchen, where Molly and I have spent many hours visiting, researching, and discussing paranormal problems.

I'm delighted by the surprise. But as soon as Molly shifts the camera and I see Violet, my heart sinks a little. I know she's been sick on and off, but today she looks awful. Her face is drawn and wrinkled, eyes pinched. She normally dyes her hair outrageous bright colors to celebrate different times of the year, but now the latest dye-job is growing out, leaving pale green streaks mixed with wisps of white.

Catching myself, I smile, hoping my alarm didn't show. "Hello, Violet. Great to see you!"

She smiles back. "Wonderful to see you, Abby dear."

When I ask how she's feeling she insists it's much better. "But I did want to mention something to you, Abby. I've already said this to Molly, but she wanted to make sure you heard it from me." She laughs. "I think she might be afraid I'll change my mind again."

"No ..." Molly says.

Violet raises her fingers. "It's true. I've been going back and forth about things a lot lately, and I know I've driven poor Molly crazy with it."

I must be looking puzzled, because Violet goes on: "I know, I need to explain. I'm talking about all of the Circle of Harmony writings. Molly and I have been working on them together for a long time now, trying to sort out what we might publish and how to approach that. And I've given Molly a lot of trouble by being indecisive about what pieces we should or should not disclose. Well, I've finally decided I need to let that go and stop being such a pain in the ass. So, going forward, I'm leaving it to Molly's discretion as to what to publish.

"Now, that's with two provisos: one, that she use her best judgment as taught by the Circle"— Here, Violet points to her forehead, then to her heart—"analyzing first with the mind and then listening at the heart, to confirm that the decision aligns with the Five Principles. Molly is an initiate, and I know I can trust her to do that."

The Five Principles align with the Fountains: Love, Endurance, Balance, Amity, and Bliss. They are meant to guide important decisions on the path of true magic.

"You mentioned a second proviso?" I ask.

"Oh yes. That is, if Molly is in doubt about any decision, that she consult you, Abby. I could have named Kevin or your grandmother, but I wanted it to be someone young, and you are the obvious choice. Is that okay?"

"Of course."

"Well, that's a relief, I don't mind telling you," Violet says. "Now, I fully intend to keep working with you both, and helping you interpret any of the Circle knowledge you wish to pursue. But I feel much better letting go of the responsibility for choosing what gets shared with the world. And I know I am leaving the Circle's traditions in trustworthy hands."

It strikes me that Violet has come to this decision because she's thinking she might not be around much longer. Naturally, we all knew this already. She is in her late seventies, after all.

And this doesn't mean she's dying anytime soon, I tell myself. She'll hopefully live a lot more years.

Still, this conversation is breaking my heart.

The first night I met Violet, I was in deep psychic trouble, haunted by what I thought were hallucinations, sure I was losing my mind. Grandma brought me to Violet and Kevin's house. Violet read tarot, analyzed my situation, assured me that the haunting was real. She introduced me to the Circle of Harmony, taught me the Principles, led my initiation. She has guided me at each step of my crazy, magical journey. When she's gone, hopefully Kevin and Grandma will be there to carry on the Circle, but Violet has been our leader, our psychic center—irreplaceable.

After a few seconds, Molly clears her throat and leads us past the awkward silence. Based on what Violet has said, and given how little progress she and I have made with the sigil magic, Molly suggests switching gears and working instead on the history of the Circle.

"There's plenty of work to do on that," she says. "Heck, with all the material we've got, we could probably produce two or three volumes. Would you be willing to help, Abby?"

"What would you want me to do?"

"Research some of the historical accounts, review stuff I've written, whatever you have time for. I know you have lots going on."

Well, that's an understatement. I mumble an answer: "Sure. I'd be happy to help, time permitting."

Violet asks how things are for me. Has there been any recurrence of "that demon problem."

I breathe in before answering. I want to spill it all, tell them what happened on the Bridge of Lions last night, recount my talk today with Jeremy. Molly would certainly be interested. She'd want more information, especially about the 'demon battle as VR game' idea. But she'd also be perplexed and worried for me. As for Violet, she wouldn't understand the game angle at all. And the last thing I want to do is add to her stress.

So I just tell them things have been a little up and down, but it looks like a solution might be coming.

After we end the call, I stare at my phone, feeling deflated and lonesome.

〰〰

But I can't afford to wallow in misery. I have a demon to banish. Plainly, this has become my job, whether I want it or not.

The question now is: should I agree to play Jeremy's game? Will this really keep Alyas occupied so he's not harming anyone else? Might it teach me more about the demon, help me find a way to defeat him?

Or would I just be playing into their hands?

Hard to fathom. The more I sit and think about the problem, the more paralyzed I feel.

Gotta snap out of it!

I haven't had any lunch. Can't fight monsters on an empty stomach. I fix myself a peanut butter sandwich and cup of tea. After eating, I feel a bit better.

Sitting comfortably on my bed, I meditate, then move into the Daily Ablution exercise. I spend extra time envisioning each Fountain, letting the mystical waters soothe me.

Calmer now than I've felt all day, I pick up my seeing stone. Holding the necklace by the silver chain, I let the topaz hover in front of me, staring at the sharp angles of dark and light.

No definite answers appear, so I try again, this time framing a question: *What will happen if I agree to play the game?*

Eventually, there are glimpses, fragments like dreams: winding stairways, long painted corridors, paths through dark, humid woods. Always I'm hurrying, struggling, desperate.

That's how I spend the rest of the day and the next: locked in my tiny apartment, depressed, struggling to raise enough energy to see my way clearly.

Tuesday is July 4th. In Harmony Springs, most of the town gathers for a picnic in Founders Park. Molly's family will be there, maybe Grandma. Kids will run around kicking soccer balls, throwing frisbees. After dark, they'll shoot off fireworks over the river ... Harmony Springs, the peaceful little town I call home. I would be there now, if I hadn't chosen this internship. Maybe St. Augustine is just not for me. Maybe Grandma is right, and I should pack it in and go home.

But each time that impulse rises up, I know it won't happen. My mom would be ashamed of me. Worse, I'd be ashamed of myself. No matter how tough things have gotten in my life, I've never been a quitter.

But I need answers.

The seeing stone hasn't helped. The Daily Ablution has not brought me any visions or guidance, as it often has in the past. Finally, I fall back on the technique Violet mentioned: analyze with the head, then listen with the heart.

Sitting at my keyboard late Tuesday afternoon, I set out to analyze. I've learned a lot in my pre-law courses and internship about legal analysis—weighing a problem from different angles, seeing pros and cons, asking penetrating questions. Before I agree to play the game, I should gain as much information as possible, interrogate Jeremy like a lawyer.

After I've listed all of my questions and possible ramifications, I read them over. Then I listen with my heart.

Then I log in to the gaming site and send RJWizard a message: "I may be willing to play, but first I have questions."

After a couple of hours, he sends a meeting link.

"Alyas knew you couldn't resist," Jeremy tells me with a smirk.

"Questions first."

"Go right ahead."

"Tell me about the demon. Everything you know."

When he hesitates, I add: "Do you want me to play the game or not?"

"All right. As best I understand it, he draws his existence from the human race, like the collective unconscious, you know?"

This fits what the demon himself told me, in my vision of the place of slaughter. And it matches some of my own experiences. When I've faced monstrous spirits in the past, they were born, in one way or another, from human thought and emotion. The first one, named Raspis, was manifested by the unconscious minds of three initiates of the Circle of Harmony. The other, Ranee Virum, was spawned from an internet meme.

"So he's like a thought-form then?"

"Something like that," Jeremy agrees. "But he's also attached to the land, specifically the area around the Matanzas inlet. I think he's been here as long as there have been humans. But he's told me his power increased with the arrival of Europeans. You've heard of the slaughter of the French Huguenots?"

"Yes..."

"That was like a birthday bash for him. After that, he grew stronger. Later, he managed to tempt some Spanish priest, who dabbled in alchemy, to summon him. That scene's gonna be in the game."

Another vision I've seen. But what I really need to learn are the demon's strengths and weaknesses. How to get inside his head and thwart him, if I can. I'm smart enough to know I can't just ask Jeremy that. Have to work him around to it.

"And how did you first get in touch with Alyas?"

"Okay, so I was trying to think up a new game, something different and spectacular. I knew I needed an adversary, and a magical demon seemed like a good bet. But the more I tried to make him original, the more flat and unimaginative he seemed. I got more and more frustrated, but I didn't give up. Then one night, he just came to me. I was writing dialog for the demon and, it was like it started writing itself. After that, I began hearing his voice in my head, and later, I started to see him—first out of the corner of my eye, then plainly in the room with me. By then, I knew I hadn't created him, but *discovered* him."

Sounds like how a demon might work his way into a susceptible mind. "And has it occurred to you how dangerous this is? How, likely you are to end up one of his victims?"

Now Jeremy looks defensive. "Nah, I don't think so. He needs me, to create the game. And it's going to be spectacular. A game like no one has created before."

"Okay. About the game: how will it work exactly? You're proposing that I play against the demon, but what does that mean? And how is that going to translate into a game that other people can actually play?"

Jeremy nods, enthusiastic. "Yeah. I admit, I'm still working on that part. But basically, players will face the demon at different points in the history of St. Augustine. Alyas will be about to do something evil, and it will be up to the player to stop him. And that's where you come in, COH Girl. You'll try to stop him with some of that magic you're so good at. Alyas will fight back. If you are able to defeat him in that particular time and place, I'll adapt whatever magic technique you used and code it into the game, so it becomes available to future players to discover. You'll be our co-author, in a way."

"Really?"

"Yeah. Don't get me wrong, I'm not offering to pay you for it. Well, I guess if the game ends up making *a lot* of money, I could cut you in."

"Never mind that. What I want to know is, how playing this game is going to help me banish the demon *in real life*. Like drive him away from our world?"

Jeremy shrugs. "That's for you to figure out. I only said the game would keep him occupied and that he promised not to do any more damage while you're playing. But who knows? Since it really will be Alyas playing against you, maybe you'll learn what his weaknesses are."

Bingo. "Which you know already?"

"Nope. Haven't a clue. That's why I need you to play the game. Like I said, I'm just the programmer."

Is he lying? I don't sense that he is. He doesn't know any more than he's told me. Which means, if I'm going to discover how the demon is vulnerable, I'll have to do it on my own. Which means ...

Analysis time is over. I check once more with my heart.

And the answer, like it or not, is: "All right. I'll play the game."

That smirk again. "I knew you would! Level 1 will be ready in a few days. I'll be in touch."

♒

Canary Greene smiles awkwardly in the video. She's standing by some trees, leafy branches hanging down, a pond in the background. The video came as an attachment to a text she sent me, labeled with one word: "Update."

"Hello, Abby. I thought I should get in touch and let you know that, well, I've vamoosed out of St. Augustine. After that night on the bridge, it was just more than I could handle. So I quit my job and came back to my mom's place here in Lake Sylvan ..."

The name rings a bell. Small town out in the country, thirty or forty miles from the coast.

"I feel stupid about it—running home to mommy after trying so hard to be an adult and live on my own. But I didn't take demons into account when I made that plan. Anyway, I'm pretty sure my mom's protections will keep me safe here, so you shouldn't have to worry about me. And thank you again for what you did. My sister, Hummingbird, wanted to thank you too. And I'm sorry I won't be there to help you deal with the demon. Although, honestly, I don't know what help I could have been. Anyway, good luck, and take care of yourself."

Smiling awkwardly again, she shuts off the phone.

Well ... It's a relief that Canary is out of town and most likely safe from the demon. Briefly, I wonder again if it might not be wise for me to flee also—back to Harmony Springs, where Alyas' power would be far away and the magic of the Springs strong and protective, where I would most likely also be safe.

But no. That's not for me. Canary could not do anything else about the demon except to run.

But I *can* do something.

And so, I must.

12. Ready Player COH Girl

Level 1 is ready on Friday.

I get a text from Jeremy late in the afternoon. Being at work, I don't want to open the link. Instead, I log into the site and send him a message:

"I'll be available at 7:30 tonight."

Around seven, having rested and eaten a little dinner, I meditate and perform the Daily Ablution. After centering and calming myself as much as possible, given the circumstances, I open the closet where I keep my magical tools. Each is wrapped in a silk scarf: wand, dagger, cup and seeing stone. Carefully, I unwrap each tool and place it on the writing table beside my tablet. I have no idea if I'll be able to use them.

Because, really, I have no idea what I'm doing.

But fear and doubt are not going to stop me.

I boot up the tablet and log in to the site. When I open Jeremy's message, the link takes me to a video chat. After a few minutes, he comes on.

"Ready to start?"

"Yes, I am."

"Excellent. I'm going to post a link to a private server. Do you have VR glasses?"

"Uh, no."

"That's okay. You'll see the game in 2D mode then. First there'll be a title page with a text introduction. I'm still deciding what to call the game. 'Demon Slayer' or 'Demon of the Ancient City.' Any thoughts?"

"Really don't care."

"Fine. Anyway, like I said, you'll see it in 2D mode at first. But once it starts running, Alyas tells me your mind will be drawn in and you'll experience it just like real life. Like VR only better. Ready? Here comes the link."

A hyperlink rolls into the chat window. I take a deep breath and tap it. A new window zooms onto the screen.

Fade in to an image, a grayed photo of the Castillo de San Marcos. Rousing music sounds, as a title flashes in orange type: "Alyas, Demon of the Ancient City."

More photos of the historic district fade in and out as the introduction plays:

> Northeast Florida, near present-day St. Augustine.
> The demon known as Alyas has haunted this region since earliest times. With the coming of settlers from Europe, his power has grown.
> Thirty years ago, a Spanish army massacred hundreds of prisoners at Matanzas inlet, since then known as "the place of slaughter." Delighted by those murders, the demon now roams the settlement called St. Augustine.
> At a small church, Father Mendez has taken up what he believes is the study of alchemy. Led astray by the demon, he performs a forbidden ritual that results in opening a portal for the demon to enter our realm in physical form.
> Your mission, player, is to banish the demon back to the Netherworld.

In the photo, a small Spanish church draws near, then fades. My screen now shows an illustration of a basement or vault with white walls and low arches. The view moves toward a crudely rendered figure, a blocky little character typical of a video game. Except he's dressed in a black gown like a priest.

But as the camera moves toward him everything changes. Dark and light clash in my brain. I sway backward.

Now, as promised, I've slipped into a vision. Literally, I'm standing in the church cellar. I hide in the shadows, yards away from the priest. He's a thin old man, gray-haired and bearded. Candles surround him, and in front of him burns a black iron brazier. He's chanting in Spanish—no, Latin: invocations, groans, commands. The flames in the brazier dance as he stabs the air with a silver wand.

The demon rises out of the flames, growing as he floats in smoky air. His horned head touches the ceiling, He slips through the air and lands beside the priest, who watches him now, speechless with terror.

"Too late, too late," Alyas whispers. "You have summoned me, little man, and now you are cursed."

Father Mendez collapses to the floor, crying out to saints and angels to save him.

The face of the demon turns toward the corner where I'm hidden. "Ah, but I see another mortal is watching us. Come forth, human, and show yourself."

Ready Player COH Girl. I'm on.

I blink and will myself back to the physical world. For a second, I'm sitting at my table. I reach down and grab the wand.

Back in the game world, I step from the shadows and face the demon. I'm not afraid, just determined and ... excited. When I was younger, I played online games a lot. Now, faintly, I recognize the thrill.

Alyas flows toward me. His body has changed, no longer the bulky physical form, but a steaming cloud of fire and smoke. I lift the wand and make him halt.

"Stop, Alyas. I am a true magician and know your true name. You cannot resist me and must obey." With the wand I draw a circle in the air and trace a pentagram within. "I banish you from this time and place, never to return!"

With force beyond all fear and doubt
I vanquish you and cast you out!

Alyas smiles and starts toward me again.

I repeat the chant, my wand thrusting.

But the demon's not buying it. I don't have enough power. My will and wand and chant by themselves are not enough.

Alyas drifts closer, and my power starts to fade. From far away I hear Jeremy's whining voice.

"You disappoint me, COH Girl. Is that all you've got?"

I need something more. If I could invoke a formula from the Circle of Harmony. But no time for that. The demon's eyes burn into me. My brain feels like it's cracking apart inside my skull. The wand is in my hand. Can I will myself back to my world and pick up the dagger? That thought flies away as soon as it appears.

Alyas leans near my face, the smoke of him wrapping around me.

The wand will have to do. How can I draw more power with the wand?

"Back off!" I yell.

Frantically I wave the wand, tracing a circle, willing it to show as pink fire. The demon slides back, mouth opening.

Within the circle I jab eight times, leaving eight pinpoints of yellow light. I draw three lines, connecting four of the points with a thunderbolt.

The demon hangs back, startled.

The sigil is called *Might of Inanna*. With my wand I push it through the air, toward Alyas' face.

"By the power of the Goddess, the Queen of Heaven and Earth, I banish you, spirit, from this time and place. You cannot resist her power. You cannot resist her might."

The expression on the demon's face turns from shock to alarm as the sigil closes on him. Before it can touch his face, his arms thrust out of the black smoke. Hands clap above his head. Next instant, the demon's face and body, smoke and flame, are all gone.

Across the chamber, the old priest lies weeping on the floor, muttering thanks to saints and angels.

I take a deep breath. The scene changes. I am out of the trance and back in my chair, staring at the tablet screen. The 2D image of the underground chamber is back. Text flows up from the bottom of the display.

> Congratulations. You have banished the Demon at Level 1.
> Proceed to Level 2 via the Time Portal.

"Very good. Very good," Jeremy tells me. The game has vanished and the video call is back on my screen. "I think Alyas was impressed."

"Yippee." My excitement has drained to exhaustion. I stare at the wand in my hand, then place it carefully on the table.

I should ask questions, try to draw out any further information Jeremy might have. But even as I'm thinking that, Jeremy says:

"Level 2 will be ready in a few days. We'll be in touch."

With that, he ends the session.

〜〜〜

"Holy Crap!" Molly stares at me wide-eyed from the corner of the screen. "So Creepy Hacker Guy has set up a literal game of you vs. the demon, and you've already played Level 1? I miss one Thursday call with you and I'm *that* far out of the loop? Ugh!"

It's Saturday evening. Molly's texted me a while ago to ask if we could do an impromptu chat.

"Sorry," I answer. "Didn't mean to leave you out."

"I know. I know." She rakes a hand through her thick red hair. "But this is so weird. Did you learn anything useful from playing Round 1?"

"Not sure. I do realize that just beating Alyas in the game won't be enough. But I'm hoping I'll get to know enough about him that I can banish him for good."

"Right, What have you learned so far?"

I've been thinking about this on and off all day—when I wasn't meditating or doing protective magic or catching up on my law office work or grocery shopping.

"Well, the banishing spell that I've been using up till now had no effect in the game."

"So," Molly says, "maybe he's learned that trick and managed to adapt?"

"Could be. But then I drew a sigil of Inanna and that stopped him cold."

"Okay. Maybe we assume the demon can adapt to your powers, but is more vulnerable to something new?"

"Possibly. Also, those sigils are strong medicine. Maybe Inanna's power in particular is a weak spot."

"Make sense," Molly agrees. "After all, it was the sigils that helped you beat that nasty frog monster."

I'd been thinking that too. Ranee Virum was a thought-form that took the shape of a giant white frog. My quest to defeat him was what led me to Lock Tower and the sigils of Inanna in the first place.

I wonder aloud: "Maybe demons and other evil spirits are especially susceptible to Inanna's powers."

"So maybe you should practice with her sigils some more."

"Yeah."

"I wish I could help," Molly says. "I don't suppose Jeremy would give me a login to the game."

"I doubt it. Also, it might be a really bad idea." After feeling my brain cracking like an eggshell last night, I really don't want to expose Molly to the danger.

"Well, you're probably right," she says with a touch of regret. "I'll go back to researching demons and the paranormal history around

St. Augustine. Might find something useful there. Since our talk with Violet, all my research time has shifted over to the Circle of Harmony history."

"How's that going?"

"It's massive. So much interesting material. And Violet's kept her promise about not micromanaging. She's letting me sort it all and just supplying comments and suggestions."

"How's she feeling?"

"Better, I think. Seems to vary one day to the next."

I nod.

"Anyway, I've put together the first pass of an outline for *Circle of Harmony Chronicles, Volume 1*. I was going to ask if you'd look it over, but, now that I know you have this demon game to worry about ..."

"No, that's okay. Email it to me. I'll make the time."

Molly grins. "Thanks, Abby. Just don't let it distract you from protecting yourself, okay?"

"I won't. My priorities are definitely in order: demon fighter, law intern, Circle of Harmony scholar."

Molly laughs. "By the way. I've been thinking about that girl, Canary Greene? Has she had any more trouble?"

"Actually, yes." I haven't told Molly about rescuing Canary on the Bridge of Lions, or her subsequently leaving town. I do that now.

Molly goes bug-eyed again. "What? I missed all of that too! I need to hang a video recorder around your neck or something. How else can I keep up?"

"Difficult. I know."

"Well," Molly says. "At least it sounds like Canary is out of danger for now. That's good, right?"

"Yup. That's good."

13. I just feel certain you can help me

When I walk into Larry's office, Cassandra Lorenzo is already there, dressed in a flowered skirt, white blouse, and several beaded necklaces. She doesn't look happy. I guess she can tell from Larry's manner that the news is not good.

I'm carrying 140 pages of court fillings and decisions—all of the research I've done in the past two weeks. At Larry's suggestion, I've printed it all, to show Ms. Lorenzo how thoroughly we've looked into her case.

Larry waves me to the chair beside the client. "You remember Abby Renshaw, our intern?"

She sets her dark, penetrating eyes on me.

"I've just been explaining to Cassandra about the deep dive we've done, looking for cases to support her claim."

I set down the stack of papers, and he slides them in front of Cassandra.

"Abby is an excellent researcher," Larry says, "And, as you can see, she's done a lot of study. Unfortunately, as I expected, she could find no legal precedents to justify our filing suit."

Frowning, Cassandra flips through a few of the pages, not really reading them. "That just doesn't sound right to me." To my surprise, she faces me instead of Larry. "I've told you how besieged I feel in that house. In the past two weeks, if anything, it's gotten worse. Are you absolutely sure there is nothing the law can do to help me?"

Put on the spot, I summon my professional manner. "I'll defer to Larry on that, of course. I can only say that in all the cases I've read about attempts to reverse the sale of distressed properties, none of the lawsuits were won by the buyers. A few were settled out of court, but in those the damages were clear-cut, like termites or rotting foundations, and the claimants had strong proof that the sellers knew about the problems ahead of the sale."

I glance at Larry. Lips clamped, he gives me a quick nod of approval.

Disgruntled, Cassandra tosses the pages back on the desk. She looks at Larry, then back to me. "I just feel certain you can help me."

This gives me a weird feeling. Like she's saying she's certain in some psychic sense. Given my other preoccupations lately, I have to wonder if there might be something to that idea.

"Have you tried calling the seller?" Cassandra asks. "I've called her twice, but she just stonewalls me. But sometimes if an attorney calls ..."

Larry spreads his hands. "That would be appropriate if we felt we had any leverage. But as things stand—"

"Please, Mr. Sheldon. Would you at least try? I'm desperate."

Larry considers a moment, then shows a little shrug. "All right, Ms. Lorenzo. I don't see that it would do any harm to call her. Honestly though, you need to be prepared: she is just as likely to stonewall us."

I'm surprised Larry is so accommodating, giving her even more of the firm's time pro bono. Maybe she's appealed to some male protective instinct in him. or maybe he's treating her extra nice because she claims to have social media influence.

"Thank you so much," she says, rising to her feet. "I just really have the feeling you can help me."

Strangely, she's looking at me again when she adds that last part.

♒

"Thank you for agreeing to speak with us, Mr. McCormick."

It's Wednesday afternoon, two days after our meeting with Cassandra. Our office manager, Gloria got in touch with Ms. Michaels, the seller of the property. Ms. Michaels refused to talk with us and referred the matter to *her* lawyer, Andrew McCormick of Fort Myers. Larry's summoned me to sit in on the call and make notes.

"Certainly, Mr. Sheldon," McCormick's hearty voice comes over the speaker. "But I won't take much of your time. My client is absolutely not interested in taking back the house in St. Augustine, which she sold in good faith."

"I'm sure she did," Larry answers. "But unforeseen problems have arisen. Has your client informed you of the issues Ms. Lorenzo is having with the house?"

McCormick replies with a soft laugh. "Yes, I understand your client is having trouble with an evil spirit."

"In fact, she claims there have been disturbing manifestations and damage to her personal property."

This time the laugh is clearer. "Well, I am sorry to hear that. But my client tells me she actually discussed the fact that the house was haunted with your client, and your client considered that a desirable feature. However, be that as it may, you know and I know your client has absolutely no standing to bring suit in a court of law."

Larry winces. He knew this was coming. "So your client will not consider any settlement in which she resumes ownership of the property?"

"Categorically no."

"Thank you, Mr. McCormick. We won't take any more of your time."

Larry taps the button to close the call. He shows me a fatalistic smile. "Okay, Abby. I believe I can safely mix my metaphors and say we have now covered all bases and gone the extra mile for Cassandra Lorenzo."

14. Maybe the demon is playing me

Alyas, Demon of the Ancient City.
Level 2

The title fades to reveal a grainy photo that looks like an archaeological dig, with fields and scrub in the background. Superimposed text scrolls from the bottom.

> 1777. The British now rule Eastern Florida.
> South of St. Augustine lies the plantation colony of New Smyrna. Hundreds of indentured servants, collectively called "Minorcans," work under horrible conditions. Malnutrition and malaria claim many lives. The demon Alyas has gained influence over the plantation overseers, inciting brutal treatment.
> The Minorcans originally signed on for nine years of labor in exchange for passage to the New World. But the masters of the colony now insist they continue until all debts they have accrued have been paid. Alyas seeps into the minds of the desperate laborers, relishing their suffering and despair.
> Your mission, player, is to overcome the demon's influence and free the captives.

As the text fades, so does my sense of reading a screen. Last time, at Level 1, I appeared in the church basement with the demon and the priest. This time I see a series of visions, one fading to another like a movie montage—laborers in the fields sweating under a blazing sun; a scrawny, almost naked man being kicked and beaten by two overseers; a sick child crying in the dim corner of hut while adults lean near, helpless. Always, Alyas is a hovering shadow who watches with glee.

I recall enough of the history to know that the description of the New Smyrna colony is factual. But as the visions stream through my mind, I not only think they are real, I *feel* the terrible suffering. Anger and despair grow in me, at Alyas, at Jeremy, at the whole history of human inhumanity ...

I've drifted into another scene. A group of the indentured people are meeting in a dim, cramped room surrounded by stone walls. The game translates their talk into English as they argue and complain. It is more than nine years since their arrival. By the agreement, they should have been freed by now and given land of their own. They have brought these complaints to the plantation owners, only to be met by indifference or beatings.

On the far side of the room I see Alyas watching the meeting, grinning at the misery and pain.

Some of the men want to sneak away from the colony, trek overland to seek justice from the British governor at St. Augustine. Others argue against it, fearful of punishment. A woman cradles a child and weeps. I feel her emotions ripple into my heart—unbearable grief.

Then, looking at Alyas, I remember I am in the game and expected to act. I snap my mind out of the vision, back to reality, just long enough to pick my wand off the table.

After fading back to the game, I circle the room, approaching Alyas. I point my wand, trace the pentagram and the *Might of Inanna* sigil, speak the spell to drive the demon away.

Nothing happens. Not only is Alyas not bothered by my efforts, he doesn't notice me at all. His attention is fixed on the Minorcans, who are still talking and arguing, some angry, some resigned and despondent. Alyas drinks in their pain.

I try the banishing again. No effect.

What's wrong? The demon should at least be feeling my efforts. I stare at the wand, my brain dull and woozy.

The Minorcans murmur in weak, defeated voices. They do not see the demon. Only I see him.

Then I think: he's not present in any physical sense. As it said in the introduction, the demon has seeped into their minds. I can't banish him physically from their world.

But I don't need to.

Once more I step out of the game, back to my apartment. I lay down the wand and pick up the seeing stone. Shifting back to the game world, I turn my back on the demon. Mentally, I cast light into the seeing stone. Then I walk among the gathered workers, holding up the stone, casting its light into their minds.

I know the real history: The Minorcans did send representatives to the governor of St. Augustine, complaining of the conditions. The governor listened and granted their release. They left the plantations, marched north, and settled in the city.

I cast that vision into the seeing stone, and through the stone into their psyches. I can actually see the power crossing through the air, into their eyes and brains. Slowly, their expressions grow quiet, peaceful, touched by hope.

When I look over to the corner, the demon has disappeared.

Loud music sounds in my ears. I snap back to my room, the tablet in front of my eyes.

> Congratulations, Player. You have banished the demon.
> You may now proceed to Level 3.

The game closes and a video window opens with Jeremy's face. "Well done, COH Girl. I never would have thought of that, but it worked."

I just stare, too drained to think of an answer.

"I'll let you know when the next level's ready," he says. "Isn't this fun?"

〜〜

I get a decent night's sleep and feel better in the morning—still mentally drained, but not exhausted. As I go through my day at the law office, Level 2 of the game keeps coming back to me: Not just experiencing the pain of the indentured workers, or the satisfaction of overcoming the demon, but the game itself. The more I think about it, the harder it is to imagine this being turned into a game that people could actually play.

And that idea suggests a tactic I might take against the demon, one involving Jeremy.

When I get home from work, I send Jeremy a message. "I'd like to talk. Set up a chat, please?"

His response comes immediately. After taking a few moments to gather my thoughts, I open the link.

Jeremy shows me an exaggerated grin. "What's up, COH Girl?"

"Hello, JBWizard. I wanted to talk to you about the game."

"Fire away."

"Well, not sure how to say this without hurting your feelings, but having played two levels now, I don't think your game is very good."

His expression droops. "What!?"

"Granted, I haven't done much gaming the past few years. But I used to do quite a bit. It's just hard for me to see how people—who are not me—are going to play it. Or, really, why they'd want to."

Now he's offended. "I did say this is *alpha testing*, right? Do you even understand how the stages of software development work?"

"That's really not the point, because I think the whole concept is flawed. I mean, the idea of player vs. demon is good. But all that historical text in the introductions? Hard to imagine players being interested enough to read it."

"It just requires a little intellectual curiosity!" He's shouting now. "Plenty of gamers have that."

"Well … maybe. But the scene last night? Do you think normal gamers are going to want to experience all that suffering? Or that they'll stick with it long enough to figure out that the solution is to make the people hopeful—never mind finding a way to do that?"

"I told you, we are using your ideas for some of the magic. That's why you were selected for the alpha tests. Did you pay attention to *anything* I said?"

He did say he was planning to code my solutions into the game. But I really can't see that working for other players. Besides, from the way Jeremy is reacting, I'm even more convinced that the game is a fraud, that Alyas is playing on Jeremy's delusions.

But can I make him see that?

"I understand everything you're saying, Jeremy. But I just don't see it working. You think you're collaborating with Alyas. But has it occurred to you that he might be playing you, deluding you just like he did the Minorcans in the story last night?"

For a second he looks startled, like my idea might be sinking in. But then his face hardens. "I see what you're trying to do. You want me to give up partnering with Alyas, in hopes of weakening him. Well, it won't work. I have plenty of confidence in my abilities both as a programmer and game designer. And this game is going to be a huge success. Players won't be able to get enough of it. You just keep playing. You'll see."

Abruptly, he reaches down and shuts off the meeting. I'm left staring at a blank screen.

So much for my clever plan of dividing Jeremy and the demon.

∿∿

Not very hungry, I fix a salad for dinner and eat it while looking through some law work. But concentration is hard, my mind clouded by the lingering emotions of suffering from the game.

My regular Thursday session with Molly is set for 8 p.m. As soon as I log in, she picks up on my mood.

"You okay, Abby? You look kind of dragged out."

"Excellent description, as usual." I tell her about last night's game session and this afternoon's chat with Jeremy."

"Wow," Molly says. "I didn't know about the Minorcans. I'll have to look that up. Actually, if he's building the game with scenes from different times in history, it might be more helpful to know what the next one is. Then I could look into that and maybe find something that will help you."

"I don't know what the next scene is. I guess I could try to find out."

"Good." Molly looks concerned. "Can you think of anything else I can do to help?"

I think about that. When I've been in trouble like this in past, one thing I've always done is go to Violet for a reading and advice. "Maybe another session with Violet?"

Molly presses her lips shut. "Not a good idea right now. She's needing to rest."

"Oh, no."

"Yeah. Hopefully she'll be okay in a few days. She was working pretty hard with me on the Circle of Harmony history papers."

"Yeah. How's that going? I'm sorry I haven't had a chance to look at that outline you sent me."

"Don't worry about that. It's already changed anyway."

We're both quiet for a while.

"I also got in some research on demons and the occult history of St. Augustine," Molly says. "Pretty grim stuff."

I know that's true. Being such an old city, St. Augustine has a long history of paranormal happenings, lots of it evil.

"Remember we were theorizing about the demon gaining power over people by leveraging something already inside them?" Molly says. "I didn't find any particular mention of that, not overtly. But some of the stories seemed to support the idea."

That makes me think again about the Minorcans and their masters, how Alyas fed on their emotions and twisted their actions by tapping their inner beings.

I think out loud: "I have to be careful about him doing that with me."

"Right. Have you analyzed how he *could* be doing that with you?"

I pause, look inward. "The only thing that comes to me is that I have this ambivalence about the whole magical side of my life. I mean, more than once I've put it aside, let myself get distracted by other things, not put all the work into it that I knew I should. That happened after my first summer in Harmony Springs, and it's happened again the last year or so. But every time I let it slip and focus on so-called *normal* life, something terrible comes along and zaps me—some problem I can only deal with by using magic."

"The path of true magic calls you to certain duties," Molly says, citing one of the basic lessons from the Circle of Harmony writings.

"Right. And part of me resents it. That part just wants to live a normal life."

"Same dilemma as Canary Greene," Molly points out.

"Yes. Very perceptive. I hadn't thought of it, but it's funny how she and I mirror that same conflict to each other. In her case, she grew up surrounded by magic, her mother a witch. Canary found it all crazy and unbalanced, and she rejected it. My mother's the complete opposite. She is totally wrapped up in the material world and wouldn't know a magic charm if it manifested as a bird and bit her on the nose ..."

Molly laughs. "Right. All of your magic comes from the Renshaw side."

"Yeah. That's it. My grandma and dad and the whole Renshaw line, full of magical talent. That's where my conflict is! I'm split between earthly, high-achieving Mom, who raised me, and all the psychic Renshaws. I need to guard against the demon exploiting that somehow ..."

Molly watches me as I ponder this. It brings up another disturbing thought.

"You know, I tried to get Jeremy to see that the demon might be playing him. But now I'm starting to wonder if the demon might be playing me. By my doing the game he's learning about my skills and magical tools."

"That's scary," Molly says. "Maybe you should quit the game."

"Maybe I should ... I agreed to play because I hoped it would help me learn more about the demon and spot any weaknesses. And I am learning about him, I think. But it's also supposedly a way to keep Alyas busy, so he's not working harm on innocent bystanders." I lift my shoulders. "So, I don't know, Molly. This would be a good time to visit Violet for a reading."

"Maybe in a few days."

"Yeah. Keep me posted on how she's doing. Meantime I'll do some readings on my own."

〰〰

I have to hunt through some still-unpacked luggage, but I finally find my tarot cards. I shuffle and lay out several spreads, but no definite guidance appears. I'm presented with wands and swords crossing in odd places, *The Devil* (of course), the chaotic destruction of *The Tower Struck by Lightning*, the uncertain journey represented by *The Moon*.

Confusion.

Making sense of tarot readings is another skill that I've let lapse.

I finally give up. After some yoga and a shower, I feel more relaxed. I sit on my bed and do the Daily Ablution.

When I reach the third Spring, my mind is elevated into a vision. I see the Fountain of Balance as two silver basins, the water in two arcs flowing back and forth. No spirit guide appears, but I sense the lesson plainly enough: the split lies deep inside me: my ambitions to succeed in the world versus the duties of spiritual work. Both are essential parts of my psyche. I need to accept both and bring them into balance.

I empty my mind, breathe slowly, and stare for a long time at that Fountain.

When I finish the Ablution, I am warm and sleepy, completely relaxed.

But I still don't know whether or not to keep playing the damn demon game.

15. You seem determined to spoil all of my fun

Next day starts out pleasantly normal. I get up early for a run, have a shower and breakfast, make it to work in plenty of time.

Late morning, I attend a staff meeting. Gloria the office manager reviews the attorney's schedules and the status of open cases. Last in the queue, she mentions that Cassandra Lorenzo called again this morning.

"She requested another meeting with Larry. Oh, and she also asked that Abby be present."

Everyone looks at me in surprise. I'm sure the surprise shows on my face too.

"That woman needs to learn to take *No* for an answer." Teresa, the senior partner, looks pointedly at Larry.

He throws up his hands. "I called her the day after we spoke to the seller's attorney. I said I was sorry, but there was nothing more we could do."

"She asked me to tell you that things have gotten worse," Gloria reports. "*Manifestations* is the word she used. She said she was certain someone in our office could help her."

Larry and Teresa frown at each other. Nancy, the paralegal, stares at the table. Finally, Larry turns to me.

"Abby, would you be willing to give her a call? She did specifically ask that you be present. Good experience for you dealing with a difficult client."

Yeah, I think he's said that before. "Um, sure."

"Just let her talk. Listen sympathetically," Larry says. "Then report back to me—especially if you think there is anything new that might give her legal standing."

"Yes. Okay."

"But don't make any promises," Teresa warns me.

"No. Of course not."

〰️

"Hello, Ms. Lorenzo. This is Abby Renshaw with the Law Firm of Sheldon and Bond. Larry Bond asked me to return your call."

I waited till after lunch to call her. Didn't want to try this on an empty stomach. Now, comfortably dosed up with chicken salad and iced tea, I've closed the door of my closet-office and punched in the number.

"Yes! Abby, I am so glad you called. Thank you!"

I check my notes. "You have some message for Larry, regarding the house?"

"I certainly do. The infection keeps getting worse. As you know, at first there were noises and just a general atmosphere of evil. Then I started to see the entity's shadow. Then it overturned my bookshelf. But in the last week I've started actually seeing the creature. It's a demon, definitely a demon."

The fine hairs on the back of my neck prickle.

"Uh, can you describe it exactly?"

"Hulking creature, shiny orange skin, small head with horns, red eyes."

Alyas.

"I know this is not the kind of problem one normally brings to a law office," Cassandra goes on. "And I know you and Larry have been very kind to meet with me and listen. But, as you know, I am an experienced psychic. I've dealt with occult manifestations often. But never anything as strong and terrible as this demon."

"I understand ... what you're saying." *What am I going to do here?*

"I'll also say this, Abby. Being a very psychic woman, I had a strong sense that your office could help me. At first, I thought it would be to undo the sale and get me the hell out of this house. But after that last meeting with you and Larry, and now that I'm speaking with you on the phone, I think that somehow it's *you* who can help me."

Of course she does. She senses that I'm a magician and have also dealt with occult manifestations. What *am* I going to do here?

"Do you think you could at least come over to the house and see what I'm talking about?"

Duties of a true magician, as Molly said. Even in my internship, they won't seem to leave me alone.

"Umm. Let me be clear: I cannot come to your house as a representative of Sheldon and Bond. But I can come over after hours, if you wish."

"That would be amazing!"

᭥

Cassandra's house stands a few blocks from the law office. Before dropping by, I drive home and pick up my dagger and wand, and also a candle and lighter. It's 5:40 by the time I've crossed back over the center of downtown and found the address. The neighborhood is similar to most of the areas on the north side of St. Augustine: narrow streets, some still with brick or cobblestone pavement, large oaks and broken sidewalks, mostly old, small houses and bungalows.

After parking across the street, I take my backpack and walk over to the house. Cassandra has hung a sign out front: "Cassandra Lorenzo - Reader and Advisor." She opens the door before I have a chance to knock.

"Thank you so much for coming." She looks me up and down as she swings the door wide.

Crossing the threshold, I'm embraced by warm, stifling air. There's a strong smell of incense, but under that, something else. The vibe is not at all welcoming.

"You can feel it, can't you?" Cassandra asks.

"I feel something."

She gives me a hesitant smile. "Let me show you around."

She leads me through the dining room and kitchen, then across the hall where a staircase goes to the second story. On the other side of the stairway we enter the living room, and I stop dead. The oppressive feeling of menace is way stronger here, and I immediately see why.

Alyas stands in the corner, silent, watching us.

"Can you see it?" Cassandra asks anxiously.

"Yes."

Her eyes dart back and forth from me to the demon. "I just don't know what to do. I've had to board my poor dog. It was driving her bonkers."

I gaze at Alyas. He smiles.

Time to try some true magic, I guess. I sling the pack off my shoulder, set it on the floor. Cassandra watches me with intense scrutiny.

"Listen, Ms. Lorenzo ..."

"Call me Cassandra."

"Listen, Cassandra. I might be able to help you here. But please understand, this has absolutely nothing to do with Sheldon and Bond. This is just me, Abby Renshaw, trying to help."

She nods. "I've got that."

I take out the wand and dagger. "Also, what I'm going to do here is secret. You must promise to never tell anyone about it—absolutely anyone, but especially at the law office."

"Of course. I promise."

"Good. Wait here."

JACK MASSA

I light the candle and set it down on the floor in the center of the living room. Squaring my shoulders, I lift the wand and dagger. With the wand, I trace a circle in the air, envision it as blue fire, and mentally extend it to the encompass the entire house and property. Next, I take the dagger and bind the circle with more force.

Finally, I face Alyas, who is still smirking.

Putting all my strength into my voice, I tell him: "Alyas, I know your true name. And you know who I am. I wield the power of the Springs, magic you cannot resist. I now banish you from this place and time, drive you out and set a barrier against your return."

> With force beyond all fear and doubt
> I vanquish you and cast you out.
> Nor can you attempt return,
> Lest by this magic shall you burn.
>
> By the power of the Springs,
> By the One Who Shapes All Things,
> I cast you out. I cast you out.

As I chant, I gesture first with the wand, then the dagger. On the third repetition, the demon's form begins to waver.

He's still smiling, as he whispers, "Oh, COH Girl: You seem determined to spoil all of my fun."

His tone annoys me, and I pause the chant to answer him. "Why are you even here? I thought you promised no more trouble if I played the game."

He appears affronted. "That's wrong. I only promised to cause no more suicides or major damage. But this doesn't count. It's only a minor diversion."

I raise the wand and dagger. "Whatever you call it, I want you gone."

The demon sighs. "Oh, very well. I will leave now, so that I may save my strength for the game. We shall meet again, of course."

With that, his shadow rolls up like a window shade, and he is gone.

Also gone is the dank, malignant heat in the air.

Cassandra, leaning on the doorframe, her mouth hung open, stares from me to the empty corner and back again. And again.

I'm not sure if she heard the demon talking to me. She only says: "It's gone?"

I nod.

"Where did you learn to do that?"

I bend over and snuff out the candle. "I can't tell you. Secret, remember?" Standing, I point the wand at her. "And remember your promise to never speak of it to anyone."

She walks over like she wants to hug me. "Of course, I promise." She glances once more into the corner. "I sensed in the office that you are an old soul, Abby. But I had no idea ..."

As I'm putting my gear away, she asks, "Can I offer you something to eat?"

〰

Not having had dinner yet, I accept the invitation. Cassandra fixes herbal tea and tuna sandwiches with chips. We sit in her kitchen with the afternoon sunlight shining behind the back windows.

"I'd really love to chat with you about your magic, Abby. I know your story must be very intriguing."

Mouth full of sandwich, I hold up a hand. "I'm sorry. I really can't talk about it. Secrecy is very important."

"Oh, I understand. And you needn't worry about my keeping my promise ... I just wish there was something more I could do to thank you. If you'd ever like a reading ..."

"Sure. I'll keep that in mind."

She's smiling. "The house feels so much lighter. I can't tell you what a relief you've brought me."

I feel really happy about that. However ... "I should tell you, though: I've banished the demon from your house for now. But it's possible he could return."

"Oh?"

"Yeah." I take out my phone. "Let me send you my number. If he gives you any more trouble, please don't call the law office. Call me personally."

"I will. Thank you so much."

Cassandra gives me her cell number. As I text her mine, I wonder again why Alyas manifested here in the first place. Is he pursuing other "minor diversions" around town? Or did this have something to do with Cassandra's connection with Sheldon and Bond, and therefore with me? Another way to draw me out, to play me?

And where does that leave me in terms of whether or not to continue the game?

From all I've been able to tell, the demon *has* kept his word about not causing any more suicides or major damage while the game goes on.

Even if that only *might* be true, do I have any choice except to keep playing?

16. A witch, and three more witches

Alyas, Demon of the Ancient City
Level 3

1821. An epidemic of yellow fever sweeps St. Augustine.
Madame Galanis, a wise woman of Greek descent, has already
seen her husband die. Now her seven-year-old son Nikos is
succumbing to the deadly disease.
Having prayed to the Christian God and saints to no avail,
Madame Galanis prepares to conjure a demon in hopes of
saving her only child. Alyas watches, enjoying the woman's
suffering and eager to be summoned.
Your mission, Player, is to overcome the demon's power and
keep him from entering our world.

As the text vanishes I am drawn into the scene: a small bedroom
under a low ceiling. Light from an oil lamp reveals a child, stiff and
moaning, lying on bed against the wall. His skin has a gray-yellow
shade. Dark blood trickles from his nose. The air is stagnant and hot.

A short woman dressed all in black stands in the center of the
room. She holds a crooked wooden wand in one hand, her arms
spread wide. A circle of yellow flame hovers in the air around her.
Alyas waits in the doorway, just outside the circle.

The woman starts to chant.

Wand in hand, I slide through the yellow fire to stand between
the wise woman and the demon. Pointing the tip at Alyas' face, I
trace a banishing pentagram and order him to leave.

The demon laughs. His huge paw swings up and knocks the wand out of my hand. Shocked, I come awake in my apartment.

The game scene displays in 2D on my tablet. I hear the woman chanting. I know Alyas is moving closer to her. Desperate, I look around for my wand and spot it lying on the floor. My gaze sweeps back to the other tools, placed on the table beside the keyboard.

I pick up the cup and will myself back into the game. Veils of light and shadow move past me. I find myself standing in the corner of the bedroom. I have to interrupt the woman's invocation.

On the wall hangs a picture, an icon of a woman with a halo—the Virgin Mary, I believe. I pull the icon down, rush through the circle of fire and stop in front of Madame Galanis. I thrust the icon before her eyes. Her mouth drops open and she stares, speechless.

Behind my back, Alyas hisses.

The woman's hands come up to grip the icon. I sense she cannot see me, only the picture and my cup floating in the air. I touch her elbow, turn her, steer her to the bedside.

Gazing at her sick child, she clutches the icon to her heart and drops to her knees in prayer. I lean past her, holding the silver cup over the child's head.

One of the functions of the Cup of Amity is healing. I invoke that power now.

I can feel the yellow fever pulsing from the boy's body, wave after wave of gray, slimy energy. Some of it touches me, seeps into my pores, but I ignore it. I focus on visualizing the pure water of the Springs, flowing from above, filling the cup and then pouring over the sick child.

Deliberately, with all my will power, I send the healing magic over his scalp, into his brain, then down his spine and out to every part of his body. Beside me, Madame Galanis sobs and prays.

It takes a long time, but slowly the boy relaxes. His breathing comes easier. His face takes on an expression of peace. Even his skin color looks less yellow.

When I straighten up and look behind me, the demon is gone.

♒

"Oh, that was very good. VERY good!" The text from Jeremy is on my phone the next morning. "Defeating the demon by halting the invocation and then healing the child yourself. I NEVER would have thought of that!"

After leaving the game last night. I could hardly stand up. My head ached and I could hear blood throbbing in my ears. Lingering effects of the child's sickness, I guess, and the magic I used to wash it away. I didn't even bother to undress, just shut down my tablet and phone and crawled into bed.

I woke up before seven, daylight filling the apartment. I slept over ten hours but still felt weak and exhausted.

But today is Monday. I have to be at work.

So I climbed out of bed, showered, then put on the coffee pot and booted up my phone.

Below the text from Jeremy I see two from Molly.

Oh, no! When I got the game invite last evening, I totally forgot our Sunday video call.

Molly at 8:10 last night: "Aren't we supposed to meet tonight?"

Molly at 8:45: "Are you all right?!"

I text her back: "Sorry. I got tied up last night. Meet Thursday as usual?"

A few minutes later, while I'm gulping down my coffee, she replies: "You okay?"

Actually, I feel terrible. Like I'm coming down with the flu. I give her a short answer: "Tired. Talk soon."

As the day goes on I feel worse: splitting headache, sore throat, sniffles. I'm sure it's some sort of magical backwash from the healing I did in the game. Could I actually have yellow fever? In a surge of paranoia, I look up the symptoms. Mine are close, but not exact.

Besides, yellow fever is extremely rare now and is caused by mosquitoes.

So probably not.

Still, I feel increasingly miserable and can barely concentrate on my work.

After lunch, Larry stops by my desk. He asks how I'm feeling, and I tell him I might be catching a cold.

Then he says, "By the way, I heard from Cassandra Lorenzo this morning. She wants us to hold off on any legal action. She says things at her house are much better and that, quote, 'Abby seems to have solved the problem.'" He looks at me in confusion. "I know I asked you to call her on Friday. So I have to ask: How exactly did you solve her problem?"

"Oh." I look down, touching my forehead. I didn't ask anyone's permission to go to her house (and I'm glad she didn't mention that part). What can I say here that won't get me into trouble? Sometimes a magician's life calls for little white lies.

"Well, I called her like you asked, and I managed to convince her to chill out about it. I guess she just needed someone to hear her out and listen sympathetically."

Larry seems mystified.

"It might not last," I add. "I can't promise she won't come back to us."

"No. Of course not." Larry smiles. "Anyway, great work. And you might want to take the rest of the day off. You sound awful."

Following Larry's advice, I head home early. By the time I climb the stairs to my apartment the symptoms are terrible, like the ugliest cold I can ever remember. I skip dinner, just drink some juice, shut off my phone, and go to bed.

〰

If anything, next day is worse. I'm feverish and hurt all over. I call in sick to the office and actually consider going to an urgent care facility. But the closest one is out on the highway, and I'd have to drive. Instead, I walk over to the supermarket and stock up on aspirin, cold medicine, and an herbal tea to boost my immune system. Then back home to collapse.

I'm lying in bed that evening, drifting in and out of consciousness, when my phone buzzes with an incoming call. I turned it on earlier in the day to check messages, but didn't feel up to answering them. Apparently, I forgot to shut the phone off again. Now, I think I'll ignore the call—really not wanting to talk to anybody.

But something makes me get up and answer.

The display tells me the call is from Canary Greene. I hope *she's* okay. I'm in no shape to rescue her this time.

I tap the icon and a video window opens. Canary is standing in the twilight under an oak tree.

"Hello, Abby. I hope you're okay. Have you got a few minutes?"

"Yeah. What's up?"

"Well, I hope this isn't an imposition—Just say so if it is and we won't bother you. But Hummingbird and my mom, Margaret, are here."

She moves the phone, panning to show her little sister and mother. Both of them wave, and Hummingbird, the solemn-faced child, calls out, "Hello, Abby!" They are standing beside a campfire and both are dressed in robes. The camera moves back to Canary, and I realize she too is dressed in a ... witch's robe.

"You see, Hummingbird had this vision. She thinks you might have taken a bad hit fighting the demon. My mom did a reading, and she saw it too. So we decided—with your permission—to do a spell, for protection and also healing. Because they thought you might have gotten sick ..."

"Wow." I slump into a chair, gazing at the phone.

Canary winces, looking embarrassed. "If this all sounds too crazy ..."

"No! Not at all. Hummingbird and your mom are exactly right. And I could use any magical help you can send."

"Okay!" Canary smiles, relieved.

"I told you!" Hummingbird cries in the background.

"Yes, you did, honey," Margaret says.

Canary sets her phone down, propped on something, so the camera is pointed at the fire. Margaret instructs me to sit and relax and open myself to their energy. I stare into the flames, taking slow breaths, mentally reaching for a place of calm.

After huddling together a few moments, the witches begin. They arrange themselves around the fire. Taking a wand from a pocket of her robe, Margaret paces around in a circle. She stops at each of the four cardinal points, traces a pentagram in the air and calls out an invocation to the elemental spirits—Air in the east, Fire in the south, Water in the west, Earth in the north.

All of this is familiar to me, similar to the opening of a Circle of Harmony ritual. What comes next is different. Returning to the fire, Margaret stands between her two daughters and takes hold of their hands. They raise their arms together and Margaret says:

"Lady and Lord, you who rule the Earth and Sky and are the soul and body of Nature, we now invite your loving presence into our circle. Honor our call. Come and be with us."

"Come and be with us," the two girls repeat.

Even on the little screen, in the dim firelight, I can tell that all three of the witches have gone into trance.

"They are here with us," Margaret intones.

"They are with us," Canary and Hummingbird answer.

"In this protected circle is one other," Margaret goes on, "present spiritually though not physically. Our friend, Abby, who has done us great service, who is struggling to overcome an evil one, and who now needs our strength and healing energy. By the power of the four Elements, by the Lady and the Lord, we send her healing, strength, and light!"

Hummingbird has picked up a drum and now strikes it. Led by Margaret, the witches march around the fire, chanting.

> By Water, Air, Earth, and Fire
> By the Lady and the Lord
> Power, peace, and healing light
> Power, peace and healing light!

Round and round they march, swaying to the drum beat, Margaret and Canary clapping their hands. The phone clutched in my palm quivers with the same tempo. The energy flows into me: soothing my throat and chest, releasing the sickness.

I lose count of the number of times they circle the fire. Finally, they stop and shout the verse one last time, thrusting their arms high.

Margaret ends the ritual, thanking the Lady and the Lord, then pacing around the magic circle and drawing banishing pentagrams.

Canary comes and picks up the phone. Peering into the camera, she says: "I hope that will help a bit, Abby."

I'm a little stunned, weak from my sickness and yet buzzing with the magic of the ritual. And stunned with a weird, tearful feeling of gratitude, to not feel so alone, to have someone else take up the burden and do magic for me.

"Thank you," is all I manage to say.

Canary smiles, and then the phone moves to show Hummingbird's serious face.

The little girl says, "Be well, Abby."

17. This is what happens when you turn off your phone

That night brings a deep, healing sleep. How much of the healing is due to the witches' ritual and how much to the various medications, I don't need to question.

By morning, I'm starting to feel better. Still foggy and drained, still dripping from the nose, but no longer at death's door. Turning on my phone, I scan the unanswered messages: texts from Molly, texts and two missed calls from my mom. Shut down your phone for two days and this is what happens. I text Mom, apologize and promise to call her tonight. I message Molly and ask if she wants to do a video chat this evening instead of tomorrow.

At 8 p.m. I'm sitting in front of my tablet when Molly comes on.

"Abby, you look terrible."

"Thanks. I never thought I was supermodel material but—"

"You know what I mean! Are you sick?"

"I've been better. But also worse."

I tell her how my week has gone, starting with Level 3 of the game Sunday evening. Molly punctuates the narrative with wild-eyed exclamations and a few profanities.

"So," she says, when I finish, "you defeated the demon this time by healing the sick child, so the witch woman didn't need to summon the demon after all. But you came out of the game sick yourself."

"That about sums it up."

"This just keeps getting crazier. The first two times you played the game, you came out of it feeling drained. This time you got physically sick. What does that suggest to you?"

My brain is still somewhat foggy. "I'm not sure ..."

"Well, it suggests to me that you better quit playing, before it gets even worse."

I admit I've been wondering that same thing, in my more feverish hours lying in bed and staring at the ceiling.

But I do still believe my playing the game has kept Alyas from doing more damage in the real world. And I still have hopes that, by keeping him playing against me, I can discover some flaws in his armor.

Of course, if the next round kills me, that won't help anybody.

"Abby, did you hear what I said?"

"Yes, Molly. I know you may be right."

〜〜〜

After closing the chat with Molly, I keep my promise and phone Mom. She answers right away. I apologize for the missed calls and explain that I'd been sick and shut off my phone for a couple of days.

"Oh, no! I had a feeling something was wrong."

"Just a cold, Mom. I'm better now. Planning to go back to the office tomorrow."

"How many days have you missed? Are you sure you're okay?"

"Just two days—well, two and a half. And yes, getting better."

"I'm so sorry. I really don't like you being down there all alone. I wish you were closer, then I could make sure you got proper care."

"Mom, I'm twenty years old. I can manage."

"You *would* tell me honestly if something more serious was wrong?"

Well, except for the supernatural things, which are mostly what's seriously wrong. "Of course, Mom. Don't worry."

"I'm trying not to. Have you given any more thought to your law school applications?"

That again. "Not really. The internship has been keeping me so busy. But it only goes till end of August, and according to that checklist you sent me early applications don't need to be submitted till November of senior year. That gives me all of September and October to decide on schools and write the applications."

Mom sighs. "I suppose you're right. And the last thing I want to do is pressure you when you've been sick."

I take the opportunity to change the subject and ask how things are with her. We chat about her work, and about a vacation she's planning with her husband Jim, to Canada.

After she hangs up, I mentally review our talk. Pretty sure I'm right about there being plenty of time to put together the law school applications after the internship ends. Of course, if I was a different person, I would be finding time now to at least investigate schools and plan my applications.

But that's not going to happen.

I take another dose of cold medicine and head off to bed.

≋

Next morning, perhaps inspired in part by Mom's ambitious energies, I'm determined to go back to work. Still feeling sluggish, but reasonably sure I can manage. While I'm getting dressed, I get a call from Grandma.

Her tone is anxious. "Hello, Abby. Are you feeling all right?"

Well ... "Getting over a cold, but better today."

"Oh, glad to hear that. I was worried cause I haven't heard from you lately, and I had a premonition you might be sick. Then I saw Molly yesterday in town, and she said you weren't answering her texts."

"Yeah, I had my phone off part of the time. But I talked with her last night."

"Good. I know she was worried about you too. Are you sure you're all right? Are you still having trouble with that demon creature?"

Damn. I don't want to worry Grandma, but I also don't want to lie to her. And she knows me too well to be fooled by any soft-soaping. So I confess about the last round of the game, and how the experience left me sick.

"But I am almost fully recovered now, Grandma."

"Abby, I don't like this. I don't feel good about you facing this on your own. When you had similar troubles in the past, at least there was Violet and Kevin to back you up."

"How is Violet? Molly said she was ill again."

"Yes, another relapse of her respiratory condition. Kevin says it's better the past couple of days."

"Well, that's good at least."

"I'll say this again, Abby: You can come home. Dropping out of one internship, when you're not even in law school yet, is not going to ruin your career."

"I know that, Grandma. I'll think about it, I promise."

She pauses for a second. "Another option is that I come to you. I could visit for a few days."

I don't have to think long about that to know it's a bad idea. The last thing I want is to expose her to the demon's power. "No, Grandma. If I get past the point where I can cope, I'll come back to Harmony Springs, I promise."

"Okay. I did want you to know that I could come though. I'm signing the partnership papers with Mr. Tsai tomorrow, and his daughter Amelia could cover the shop for me. She's already working on reopening Jenny's shop next door."

I hadn't forgotten about Granma taking on a partner for her antique shop. But I also haven't been thinking about it much. I know it's good to relieve her of the pressure of running the business by herself. Still, the idea makes me sad.

"Are you still good with taking on the partnership, Grandma?"

"Oh, sure. I mean, it's always hard to step back from things this way. But I know it's for the best."

♒

I manage to make it through work the next two days without acting too much like the walking dead.

I think.

Everyone in the office is kind and offers some degree of concern. They don't assign me any heavy work, mostly letting me research old cases and take notes in a couple of meetings.

Still, when I get home on Friday I am thoroughly washed out. I have yogurt and herbal tea for dinner, then just lie on the couch, staring into space.

I hate this. The demon is suffocating my life. It's messing up my law internship and smothering all my off-hours. I'm twenty years old, living in a beautiful place, with a good school record and excellent job prospects. I should be happy, enjoying life. Instead I am oppressed by an evil spirit and the obligation to find some way to banish him. "The duty of a true magician." I hate this.

My phone knocks with a text. I check it and see a message from Jeremy: Level 4 is ready, and he wants me to log in.

No way. Not tonight at least. I put down the phone and slump back to the couch.

But I can't put him off forever. I'll have to decide to either quit the game or play the next round.

How am I going to decide?

My sleep that night is wretched. I keep dreaming that I'm running, along the waterfront or over the Bridge of Lions. Again and again, I see the demon watching me. Sometimes he chases me. I run faster to escape, only to find him standing in my way.

18. A Formula to Summon a Powerful Presence

In the morning, though I feel lousy, I put on my workout clothes and go for real run—my first since getting sick. I have to stop a few times, gasping for air, but I do three miles and it clears my head.

After my shower, I eat a good breakfast, oatmeal and coffee and fruit. I cast the usual protective magic to keep the demon away from my apartment.

Then I sit down and analyze.

Should I continue the game or not? I approach the problem like a legal matter: arguments pro and con.

Pro: By continuing the game I am occupying the demon, keeping him from harming others—at least while the game continues.

Con: I am wearing myself out, maybe risking my health or even my life.

Pro: I am learning about the demon, searching for weaknesses.

Okay, so what I have I learned that may help?

Theory: the demon manifests in our world by exploiting elements of a human's psyche, some evil or weakness in his victim. What good is that knowledge? Not sure.

What else? I've overcome the demon in the game three times now. How? By invoking the power of Inanna. But that didn't work the second time.

Theory: The demon is able to adapt to and resist magic previously used against him.

How else have I defeated him? By inspiring hope, by healing.

Theory: Hope and healing counteract the demon's influence.

Problem: I can't exactly provide hope and healing to the entire population of St. Augustine. I would if I could, but ...

Con: All of my analyzing has not revealed any clear ideas for getting rid of the demon.

I take a deep breath and stare at the wall. Maybe I should just give up. Maybe I should do as Grandma suggested, leave St. Augustine, go home to Harmony Springs.

Can't do that, Abby. "The duty of a true magician."

All right. If the path of true magic won't let me off the hook, maybe *it* should show me how to proceed.

I rise from the desk chair, go and sit on the couch. Breathing slowly, I relax my thoughts, then begin the Daily Ablution. Focusing on the waters of each Springs, I let their energy flow into the centers along my spine. Sometimes in the past, when I've approached one or another of the Fountains, I've met spirit guides. Sometimes it was an ancestor, Annie Renshaw my great, great aunt, or Thomas Renshaw, her father and one of the original Founders of the Circle of Harmony. A few times it was Lebab himself, the True Spirit of the Springs, who inspired the creation of the Order. Other times, it was a goddess, who is known in our tradition as the Goddess Who Shapes All Things and who told me once, "One of my names is Inanna."

That was how I first encountered Inanna.

I could really use her advice right now. In fact, I would love the advice of any spirit guide.

But no one comes. Tired as I am, I just don't have clear enough vision.

I know that the magic of Harmony Springs is strongest in physical proximity to the springs. Am I too far away? Am I just worn out? Or is Alyas sapping my power and blocking my psychic channels?

Finishing the Ablution, I try to think what to do next. The answer that comes is, "Rest."

After all, I am getting over being sick, and I haven't taken a whole day off since I came to St. Augustine nearly two months ago. It's Saturday morning. I can take the whole weekend off if I want to. That thought by itself is a comfort.

I spend most of the day relaxing and trying hard not to think about my demon problem. I watch videos, go for a walk in the neighborhood, eat lunch at an outdoor café.

By late afternoon, I'm feeling better. And ready to get back to work.

Because I've realized it's not just my sense of duty that is forcing me down this road. It's my whole belief in myself. I'm not a quitter; I'm a fighter. That's the part I get from my mom. That's the part that won't let some creepy demon and his creepy hacker guy beat me and run me out of town.

I try the seeing stone. Holding it before a candle, I ask to be shown a vision of how best to approach my problem. It takes a while. I'm now convinced that the demon's influence is blocking my psychic vision.

But, at last, I see a few glimpses: They are circles and diagrams of pink flame floating on pale blue backgrounds.

Sigils of Inanna.

Invoking Inanna's power will help me defeat the demon.

I spend the evening in front of my tablet, staring at the sigils, committing them once again to memory, calling their power into my psyche.

Then another thought occurs. I hunt through my Circle of Harmony documents and find the one called the *Book of Lebab*. This is a basic text of spells and formulas given by Lebab himself to the founders of the Order. A copy used to be given to all true magicians who advanced though the five grades to become adepts. When I finished my last advancement rite, Violet did not have a physical copy to give me, but she and Kevin let me scan in one of their copies, so I have it in a file.

The book contains some of the purest and most potent magic used by the Circle. This might be just what I need to dissolve the demon's influence around me, so I can banish him for good. As if to confirm the thought, I come upon one of the last spells in the book: *A Formula to Summon a Powerful Presence*.

Tomorrow, I decide, I will cast that formulation and invoke the power of Inanna.

Then I will sign on to the game and face the demon—for the last time, I hope.

〰〰

By noon on Sunday I'm ready. I clear the floor space in the center of my apartment, then light four candles and set them at the points of the four directions. Beside them, I set cups of water. Finally, I add a candle and bowl of water at the center.

Using the wand, I trace a circle of protection just beyond the candles. I bind the circle with my dagger. Then, holding my phone, I reread the pages from the *Book of Lebab*.

A Formula to Summon a Powerful Presence

This formulation may be used to conjure a spirit from any sphere. By combining the elementals of Fire and Air, the adept rouses both intensity and clarity, such that even the mightiest of spirits is likely to respond. Indeed, this rite numbers among the most potent formulations given to us. For this reason, it requires an extra caution. As always, the magician must make certain their motives are pure and in accord with the Principles of Harmony. But more than this, you must be sure that the being you call is beneficent. Summoning a spirit of malign or even ambiguous character can bring disastrous results.

After rereading the instructions and chants, I set down the phone. Lifting dagger and wand, I state my intention.

"I am Fighting Eagle, initiate of the Circle of Harmony. I call upon our Friends of Fire and of Water to aid me in this rite. I seek to summon Inanna, ancient goddess of the Heavens and Earth, that I may honor her and draw down her power, in order to banish an evil spirit and restore peace and harmony in this place."

Next come the chants. As I speak them, I gesture, thrusting with the wand and dagger.

> You mighty ones of fire and light,
> From the South I call your might.
> You flowing beings of lake and sea,
> From the West I summon thee.
> By your power, by your sight.
> I call the One I seek
> I call the One I seek.

Then I speak the chant I've used before, translated from an ancient text, to invoke the goddess.

> Hail to the Lady who lights the morning sky!
> Hail Inanna, blessed daughter of Heaven.
> You who journey from the Great Above to the Great Below.
> Come to me, Inanna, first daughter of the gods!

My head whirls as I repeat the chant over and over, energy flowing up from the water and the candle flame, rising and rising, until I feel myself lifted out of my body.

I float through a sky full of stars. When the stars fade, I stand in a temple or hall with arches and painted walls. Torches hang in brackets on the pillars. Their flames flicker and dance. Ahead in the distance, I see her. She wears shining robes of white and gold, and a gold headdress. Wings of light spread out behind her shoulders. She is often pictured with a lion at her feet, but this time there are two lions. They remind me of the statues on the Bridge of Lions, and they watch me quietly as I approach.

I stop some yards away. Overwhelmed by her beauty and power, I bow.

"You have summoned me, my priestess."

"Yes, Goddess. I have need of your power."

"You have allowed my power to fade in you." She gestures toward the lions. "You must draw it back into yourself."

I see what she means. My hands no longer hold the wand or dagger. So I lift open hands and mentally call the lions.

Inanna beams at me. Energy radiates from her body. The lions stir, stand silently, walk toward me. They brush against my legs, then turn, face the goddess, and lie down.

Inanna is still smiling.

For the first time in a long, long while, I am filled with power.

♒

I blow out the candles and put them away. Some of the water I drink, the rest I pour outside.

I sit down at my work table. My phone has three texts from Jeremy, which I've ignored. Now I answer: "Ready to play."

I boot up the tablet and log in to the gaming site. Jeremy's already there, waiting for me. His message displays in the chat window.

"What took you so long? We were starting to worry."

"No worries. I'm ready now."

"Finally!"

The game window opens, showing a faded photo of a small, square building.

Alyas, Demon of the Ancient City
Level 4

St. Augustine, 1843. Malcolm Price, a sadistic warden, rules the Old Jail with an iron hand. With every prisoner that he tortures and abuses, the demon's influence grows in him, and Alyas' manifestation in our world grows stronger.
A runaway slave has been arrested after stealing food in the market. In addition to the usual flogging, Malcolm Price contemplates a more horrible punishment.
Your mission is to banish the demon and dispel his power at the Old Jail.

I pick up my dagger and wand. As the text fades, my mind is drawn into the scene. I stand in the corner of a low-ceilinged prison cell. Oil lamps flicker, their light shining on a slimy floor and moldy stone walls. A tiny window with iron bars shows gray twilight outside. A Black man lies face down on a table, chained by the wrists and ankles, crying out in agony as he is whipped by a muscular White man in overalls. A tall, slim White man in finer clothes stands watching. At his shoulder, Alyas lurks, a smiling shadow flicking in and out of view with each crack of the whip.

I have to stop this. But even as I move across the cell, the guard steps back. The slim man approaches the table. He carries a hatchet.

"Now then. I don't think you'll be doin' any more stealing without yo' hands!"

He sets the edge of the blade on one of the prisoner's chained wrists.

As he lifts the hatchet, I thrust the wand and dagger crossed in front of his face.

"Stop!"

The scene freezes. I've reset the time-frame. The men in the cell are all motionless.

Only Alyas moves, sliding toward me, then towering over me. He too is holding a hatchet. Grinning, he lifts the weapon high over my head.

My dagger-point traces a symbol: the sigil called *Might of Inanna.* It burns in the air, pink flame.

The demon tilts back, startled.

"I banish you, Alyas. By the might of the goddess Inanna, I drive you out!"

The demon's snarl shows gleaming teeth. His arm strains to move the hatchet. I cast the sigil into his face. It burns him, and he screams in pain.

Still, he does not vanish. Frantically, I redraw the sigil.

"In the name of Inanna, I drive you out. You cannot resist her power!"

But he does resist. Roaring, he sweeps the hatchet down, just missing my hands.

I burn him again with the sigil, this time on the chest. He screams in pain, raising both arms.

I draw a third sigil in the air.

Alyas stares at it for a moment, bellows, groans—and disappears.

Time slips. The men in the jail cell are moving again. I whirl to look at the jailer. His shoulders are slumped, his face confused. He glances at the hatchet in his hand, then slowly turns away. As he trudges toward the door, he tells the guard, "Release the prisoner."

Relieved, I look down at my arms.

The demon is gone, but so are my hands. Blood pours from two stumps at my wrists.

That shocks me awake. I'm back in front of my screen, still holding the dagger. A deep gash splits the flesh on the side of my wrist and across the palm. Dark blood drips over my leg.

〜〜〜

"What the hell happened to you?"

Gloria the office manager surveys me with a startled expression, then focuses back on my hand. I'm a little late for work, driving with the bandage being trickier than I expected.

I drove to the ER yesterday, after not being able to stop the bleeding with just a bandage and ice. Two and a half hours to get through the wait time, paperwork, and finally to receive four stitches.

Good thing I spent the first part of the weekend resting.

"Just a little accident," I tell Gloria, trying to sound casual.

She offers a wry smile. "Well, if you need legal representation ..."

I appreciate the humor and laugh. "Thanks, but it was totally my own fault." *Well, except for the demon in the magical VR game. But we won't go into that.*

"You sure you're up to working?"

"Sure. Absolutely." Having missed half of last week, I really don't want to not be here. "I might be a little slow typing," I admit, holding up my injured arm.

"Well, it looks like a slow day," Gloria says. "If you decide to leave early, I don't think anyone will mind."

"Thanks."

I get a cup of coffee and settle in at my desk. Have to admit it: diligent legal research is the last thing I feel up to. Previously, playing the game left me drained, tired, and then sick. Now, I am literally wounded.

And disappointed in myself. I had hoped that, with all the power borrowed from Inanna, I would be able to vanquish the demon once and for all—or at least have an easier time beating him in the game.

Instead, it was the toughest, most horrible episode yet.

As I try to focus on work, my brain keeps leaking back to my supernatural dilemma. *What am I going to do now?*

One thing I know for sure: No more of Jeremy's stupid game. *Not ever.*

I'll have to find some other way ...

19. Does anything in my life make sense?

The afternoon is quiet, so I do take Gloria's suggestion and head home at 3 p.m. That turns out to be a good thing, because I would not have wanted a devastating emotional breakdown to happen at work,

Grandma calls me a little after four. Her voice is dull and flat, and I immediately know it's something bad.

"Honey, I have sad news. Violet has passed away."

The floor drops out from under me, like I've plunged into black water.

This can't be real.

"I know, it's a shock," Grandma tells me. "Kevin said she seemed a little better yesterday. Then, in the night, she woke up with chest pains. Heart attack. By the time he got her to the hospital, it was too late."

"Oh, Grandma. I am so sorry."

"I know, sweetie. There just aren't any words, are there?"

I think back to the last time I spoke with Violet, on the video call with Molly. She made it clear she was leaving decisions about publishing the Circle of Harmony material in our hands. She was preparing us both for this day. That thought even crossed my mind at the time.

Yet, now that it's happened, I just can't comprehend it ... Ever since I came back to Harmony Springs four years ago and plunged into my crazy supernatural life, Violet has been one of the people who kept me afloat. At times, she was my surest lifeline.

Now she's gone. No more of her wise advice, no more cups of tea and tarot readings at her kitchen table, no more of her loving smile.

"We're holding a Celebration of Life, Friday evening," Grandma is saying. "Kevin's inviting all her friends from town. Then Saturday, around noon, there will be a private ceremony for Circle of Harmony initiates. We'll drop off her ashes at the mouth of Bliss Spring. That was her wish."

"Okay, Grandma. I'll be there, of course."

"Oh, I'm glad. Do you think you could get here mid-afternoon on Friday, to help me set up? We're having it at the house, and I don't know how many people ..."

"Sure. I'll take Friday off from work and leave first thing in the morning."

"I hate to ask, Abby. I know how stressed and busy you are."

"Don't even think that, Grandma. Nothing is more important to me than this."

〜〜〜

Later, I'm sitting at the kitchen table, staring at untouched food on my dinner plate, when the sound of chimes penetrates my foggy brain.

Incoming video call. I pick up the phone. Molly.

Her mouth is tuned down, face pale. "Hey, Abby. You heard about Violet?"

"Yes."

"You okay?"

"Not really. You?"

"Not really." She rubs fingertips over her forehead. "I just didn't see it coming. She's been up and down for years ..."

"I know."

"I've spent *a lot* of time with her this summer, especially since we had that video meeting with her. She seemed more and more intent on transferring information—stories, reminiscences. I recorded all of it. I'm glad I did."

"I think at some level she must have known this was coming."

"I feel like I should have known it too." Molly shakes her head, on the verge of tears. "She also gave me a bunch of old papers, ones I've never seen before. She kept them locked in a dresser and said she had forgotten them. Some of it goes back to the Founders and their first magical rituals. Violet hesitated to show me those, but then just decided to hand it all over ... Some really fascinating stuff. Except for old journals from the library, I hadn't seen much from the first generation of the Founders. This might fill in a lot of gaps, I think."

"I'm glad she gave them to you, Molly. The history of the Circle is yours to write now."

"Well, yours and mine, and however much Kevin might want to contribute, of course ... How are you feeling, Abby? Still sick?"

"Well, I recovered mostly from the cold or flu bug. But then this happened." I hold up my bandaged wrist.

Molly jerks back. "What? What happened?"

"Sliced my hand. Four stitches."

"How...? You didn't play the game again?"

Molly always was quick on the uptake. "Afraid so." I tell her about contacting Inanna and invoking her power, about foolishly thinking I could go one more round and knock out the demon.

Molly shakes her head. "Abby, why would you risk that? You *really* need to stop with the damn game already."

She's right. I know she is. "Molly, I am positive you are right."

~~~

When I get to work the next day, I am resolved to sort out taking Friday off as soon as possible. I let Gloria know right away, but I also feel I should talk with one of the partners. I've missed too much work lately. I hope to make them understand that I'm not just screwing around, that this time it's like a death in my family.

So, when I spot Teresa heading toward her office, I jump up.

"Teresa, may I have a word with you please?"

She looks surprised, but says "Sure" and leads me into her office. I close the door before taking a chair.

"What's on your mind?"

I hesitate. I don't know her as well as I know Larry, and she comes across as tougher and more abrupt. I find her intimidating. "I hope it's won't be too inconvenient, but I need to take off this Friday." As she starts a scowl, I add quickly: "A friend of the family died unexpectedly, and I need to be with my grandmother, and attend the funeral."

Her face softens. "Oh, of course. I am sorry for your loss. You'll be back on Monday?"

"Yes. Well ... That is, I think so." I mean, I should be, unless something else terrible or crazy happens.

"You're not sure?"

"Well, pretty sure."

Teresa frowns, pauses to consider, then decides to let me have it. "Abby, I am sorry for your family's loss. And the last thing I want to do is pile on you at a time of grieving. But, let me give you a little well-intentioned coaching here. If you want to be an attorney, you need to be better organized. And you need to learn to handle pressure. You have missed a lot of time the past two weeks—"

When I start to protest, she holds up her hand. "I know. First you got sick, and then you injured yourself. But both of those can be interpreted as reactions to stress. All of us have noticed that in the past few weeks you seemed distracted, not well-focused ..."

Well, yeah. Trying to hold off a demon at different points in the history of St. Augustine can be distracting. But I can't exactly say that in my defense.

"I know this job can be hard sometimes," Teresa is saying, "even for an intern. But if you're not willing and able to give it your best, it's not going to be hard, but impossible. Now, I'd like you to think about what I've said. You've got about a month left on the internship. Think hard about whether you really want to be here, then let us know next week. Okay?"

I'm flabbergasted, like slapped in the face. Teresa is obviously done with me, so I stand.

"I promise to think about everything you said," I tell her. "Thank you for being honest."

Back at my desk, I bring up the file I was reading, but the words are just electrons on a screen and don't make any sense.

I wonder if I do want to finish the internship. Or even go to law school. I wonder if anything in my life makes sense or ever will.

~~~

That night after dinner I sit down at my desk and try to catch up with office work. This is both because I feel pressured to perform better for the law firm and because I don't want to dwell on my feelings of grief and loss.

I'm able to focus for five or ten minutes at a time. Then my mind slips down into various mental streams. Remembering Violet and all she meant to me. Thinking about her upcoming funeral. About returning to Harmony Springs and sharing my sorrow with Grandma and Kevin and Molly. Also my talk with Teresa. Wondering if I have what it takes to become a lawyer. Do I even want to try? With my crazy supernatural-plagued life, is it even possible?

Stop thinking that, Abby. Get back to work.

As I'm pushing my brain into another article, my phone buzzes. I'm tempted to ignore it. But curiosity gets the better of me, so I turn it over and look at the screen.

Ariel.

I pick it up, wondering if he knows.

"Abby, good to hear your voice. Are you okay?"

"As well as can be expected, I guess. You've heard about Violet?"

"Yes. Kevin called to tell me. So sad." I'm glad Kevin thought to call him. I probably should have done it myself. Ariel got close to Violet and Kevin a couple of years back when he studied Circle of Harmony magic with them. He was living in Murdock then, still in school at Claremont State, and for a while he drove up to Harmony Springs almost every weekend.

"She was such a wonderful, magical person." Ariel's voice is soft, full of remorse.

"Yes, she was." I'm close to choking up.

"Kevin kindly invited me to the ceremony on Saturday. Will you be there as well?"

"Of course. It will be so nice to see you. We're also having a Celebration of Life dinner at my grandmother's house on Friday."

"Kevin mentioned that too. I wasn't sure if I should intrude."

"Of course you should, Ariel. Violet loved you. We all love you."

"Oh ..."

"You can stay overnight at the house. There's plenty of room. Dinner will be around six, okay?"

He pauses just a moment. "All right, Abby. I will see you on Friday then."

"Good."

"Thank you ... And in case I haven't made it clear enough, I love you too."

I put down the phone and look at it for a while, my mind replaying memories of Ariel and of Violet, my heart floating in pools of love and hurt and loss.

Eventually, I release it all in tears.

~~~

When I get home from work on Thursday I notice a red MINI Cooper parked on the street. After I've parked in the driveway and am heading for the stairs, I hear a car door slam. I turn and see a chunky, bearded man walking toward me.

I've only seen him on screen before, so he's halfway up the drive before I realize who it is.

I jump back, wondering whether to run, or stand and confront him. I choose to stand.

"What do you want, Jeremy?"

He stops a few yards away, holds up his hands to calm me down. "Just to talk, that's all. Don't get so excited."

I'm not surprised that he could find my address—him with all his hacker tricks. Plus, he said Alyas knew where I lived. I take out my phone, making the point that I can call the police, or record him on video if I need to.

"Talk. But make it quick."

He glances at the bandage I'm still wearing. "Sorry about your hand, by the way."

"I said, Quick!"

"Okay. Okay." He's looks worried. "Alyas tells me you're thinking of quitting the game."

No need to disclose that one way or the other. "Keep talking."

"Well, you should know by now you can't quit." He tries to sound snide, but it's weak.

I tap in the code to open my phone. "Anything else?"

"I'm serious. You have to keep playing." Now he seems almost desperate.

I just stare at him. "Time's up."

"Listen! If you don't keep playing, Alyas is going to hurt you. You have no idea what he's capable of."

"Oh, I think by now I know quite well what he's capable of." But in the dread on his face, I see something new. "He's threatened to hurt you too, is that it?"

Now he goes pale, unable to answer.

"Now you listen to me." I'm almost shouting. "If you're afraid of the demon, that's your problem. And you can tell him that if he comes after me again, he will be very, very sorry. You got that? Now get out of here before I call the police."

Jeremy starts to speak, then changes his mind. He turns and rumbles down the driveway to his car.

In case it may come in handy, I follow him, recording a video, making sure to get a clear shot of his license plate as he drives away.

Left standing on the side of the road, I almost feel sorry for the guy.

Almost.

20. Back to the enchanted forest

In the morning, fortified by one cup of yogurt and two cups of coffee, I cast the protection formula once more over my apartment, then carry my bags down the stairs. I'm on the road by 8:30, just in time to meet a thunderstorm moving up from the southeast. As I maneuver Veronica through heavy traffic on U.S. 1, the sky goes black and the air blows in blue-gray curtains. Rain splashes on the road and drums on the car roof.

But I'm a Florida girl and used to torrential downpours. When I was a new driver, commuting to college on the back roads, this would have worried me. Once, in fact, a thunderstorm made me lose control of Veronica, and we ended up in a ditch. Of course, that incident involved an evil ghost.

Now, as I say, I'm used to it. By the time I'm ten miles down the road, the storm has leveled off to a steady rain. The sky is lighter, traffic is lighter—and so is something else. The oppressive feeling of dark energy has lessened. The sense of Alyas' presence grows dimmer by the mile.

I haven't been away from St. Augustine since taking that little road trip to Jacksonville with Molly. I've become so accustomed to the demon's evil atmosphere that I've taken it for granted. Alyas told me once that he had *always been there*, and Jeremy said that the demon was *attached* to the area around the Matanzas inlet. His power is drawn from the ground and water of St. Augustine. I've thought of this before, but never felt it as clearly as I do now, driving away from his home base.

I avoid the Interstates in favor of the back roads. From U.S. 1, I turn east on Florida 40. The storms have passed, the day growing hot. I drive through small towns, swamps, and forests. I stop thinking about demons and focus on the beauty around me.

How privileged I've been, these past four years, to live in this glorious part of the world. How lucky to have Molly and Ariel, and my friends at school. Most of all, how very fortunate to live with my loving grandmother, and to have Kevin and Violet as magical guides. But now ... how sad I feel, with Violet's passing, knowing that part of my life is over forever.

♒

Harmony Springs' historic downtown looks the same as ever—a few square blocks, the streets lined with huge oaks, brick shop fronts and commercial buildings, Victorian houses with wraparound porches and pointy turrets. I reach Main Street just after 11:15.

Grandma planned to work at her shop till noon, so I've decided to meet her here. The shop, Glenda's Antiques, shares a building with two other businesses: Palmer's Books, owned by our friend Kevin, and the Harmony Gallery, now closed and being refurbished. I pull into a parking space in front and climb two steps to the raised sidewalk.

As soon as I open the door, Grandma sees me. She's standing behind the counter, talking with a small Asian woman who I take to be Amelia, the daughter of Mr. Tsai, Grandma's new partner. Otherwise, the shop is empty except for an elderly couple browsing through antique photos.

"Abby!" Grandma hurries from the behind the counter. "So glad to see you, sweetie." She hugs me tight, then thrusts me out to arm's length. "What happened to your hand?"

I knew she would notice it right away. The cut is healed enough that I don't need a bandage anymore, but the stitches are plain to see if you look—plain, dark, and ugly.

"It's okay, just a little accident."

A flash of deep worry crosses her face. "You cut yourself?"

"We'll talk about it later, okay, Grandma?"

She whispers, "That demon again?"

"Later, I promise."

She looks around the shop, whispers. "You're right. Not the time or place. We've tried to send you protection—as much as we could. But with Violet …"

"I know."

"Okay. Later. You're staying till Sunday morning though, right?"

I hug her again. "Yes."

Grandma introduces me to Amelia and together they show me the work in progress in the space next door. Little remains of what used to be Jenny Nesheim's arts and crafts shop. Workmen have redone the floors and painted the walls. They're currently installing new shelves and display cases. Some crates of merchandise have already arrived and are stacked in corners.

"We will be selling mostly imports," Amelia explains. "Should complement the items in Glenda's Antiques nicely, I think."

She's soft-spoken, crisp, and efficient, and I can tell Grandma likes her. But I also sense a shade of ambivalence below the surface.

Or maybe that's more the deep loss we are both feeling.

We leave a short time later, Grandma in her old Honda Odyssey and me following in Veronica. A county road takes us north from downtown, past wood-frame houses, a church and cemetery. Soon we turn onto a trail of hard-packed sand, bordered by ferns and brush, shadowed by tall oak and ash trees.

The enchanted forest. That's what I called this place when I was a child. We lived in Harmony Springs, and my dad and mom worked together in a real estate office. In the mornings, they would drop me off at Grandma's house. I would often spend the whole day with her, following her around, watching her clean house and garden and cook. When her work was done, we'd sit on the back porch swing and tell each other stories. I was a sensitive little girl, and life with my parents was intense and sometimes turbulent. But with Grandma, I always felt calm and completely safe.

I'm thinking all this as we pull up in front of the house. The air is humid and birds are chirping in the high branches. The house is three stories, with a front porch and high, gabled roof. It was built in the eighteen-nineties by my ancestor, Thomas Renshaw, and has been in the family ever since. Grandma plans to leave it to me when she passes.

We spend the afternoon getting ready for the Celebration of Life dinner. Most of the food will be catered, but Grandma bakes homemade cookies and biscuits. More than forty people have been invited, Violet's neighbors, a few of her friends from out of town, people she's done tarot readings for over the years. Grandma emphasizes that the dinner will be "secular in character." The actual funeral will take place tomorrow noon, when we scatter Violet's ashes at the source of Bliss Spring. That ritual will be for Circle of Harmony initiates only.

"Of course, it's important to give everyone a chance to remember Violet and mark her passing," Grandma says as I help her dust the living room. "And her and Kevin's house is just too small, so of course I said we could hold it here ..."

She's flustered, pressured by all the preparations. I've already vacuumed the downstairs and helped her clean the kitchen. But we still have a lot to do: setting tables, laying out silverware, fixing coffee and iced tea. Still, I convince her to sit down and take a break.

"Sorry to be griping," Grandma says. "It's not about the dinner. I'm really just heartbroken. My best friend gone, my store changing in front of my eyes, and thinking about you going away next year ... Just feeling sorry for myself, I suppose."

I sit down and give her a hug. She shakes a little and sniffles. "You're such a good girl, Abby."

After another minute, she grunts to clear her throat, then sets her shoulders. "Now let's get back to work"

〜〜〜

Molly arrives a bit after five, bringing condolences from her family and a plate of muffins and scones donated by Springs of Coffee, the shop where she works. She immediately asks if I'm okay and if I'm keeping my pledge not to play any more of the demon game. When I assure her that I am, she looks relieved.

"Good. I've found something that might actually be helpful. We can talk about it later."

While she's helping us make final preparations for the dinner, Kevin arrives. He's dressed in a suit and tie, shoulders slumped, narrow face looking totally worn out. He's carrying a brass urn, which contains Violet's ashes. After he's set the urn on the fireplace in the living room, Grandma and Molly give him hugs and words of sympathy.

When it's my turn, Kevin embraces me and thanks me for making the journey.

"I couldn't miss it," I whisper, grief straining my voice.

He looks me over, his expression sad and distant. "Don't let me forget, before you leave, I have something for you. I'll bring it tomorrow to the ritual."

Two guys from the catering company ring the doorbell. They carry in trays of sandwiches and bowls of salads and set them on the tables in the dining room. Not long after that, the first guests filter in. I help Kevin and Grandma and Molly greet them and show them around the downstairs. A few of them are people I've met before in town, but most are strangers to me. After the long day and everything else I've been through lately, I'm really not in the mood to play hostess, but I do my best.

Then Ariel shows up. He's wearing a white dress shirt, slacks, polished shoes. He shakes hands with Kevin and Grandma, hugs Molly and then me. For a moment we don't say anything, just look into each other's eyes, nod. We both know what the other's feeling.

After six, when the guests have all gathered, Kevin says a few words, thanking everyone for attending, thanking Grandma for graciously offering her home. He invites anyone else who wishes to address the group to do so, and a handful of older people come up and speak about Violet and how much she meant to them. After that, people spread out to the other rooms, talking in small groups, sampling from the buffet.

Molly and Ariel and I stick together. After we've eaten, I invite them out to the back porch. We sit on the old swing and gaze off across the yard in the late-afternoon light. Beyond the trees, we can just hear the waters of Bliss Spring flowing past. Tomorrow, we will walk to the source of the spring and cast Violet's ashes into the water.

The three of us are quiet for a long time. Finally, Molly says: "I still can't believe she's gone. Even while she was sick, she always felt so full of life."

"That's it exactly," Ariel says. "Hard to accept."

"I really think she knew it was coming though," Molly adds. "I told you how the past few weeks she was urgently digging out more and more old papers to give me. By the way, I found something in one of them that might actually be helpful against the demon."

"Demon?" Ariel says. "Excuse me."

"Oh!" Molly's hand flies up to her lips. "Sorry!" She looks at me helplessly.

"It's okay," I tell her. "It's Ariel."

He *is* an initiate of the Circle, as well as a student of other kinds of magic.

"There's a demon?" Ariel asks.

I give him a short-story version of my demon summer. His face flows to different pictures of surprise, concern, apprehension, shock.

Then comes a shade of anger. "I can't believe you went through all this without telling me! You should have let me know."

"I would have, Ariel, if I'd thought there was anything you could do. But things kept taking strange turns and ... I didn't know what was coming next."

He squeezes my hand. "I don't know what I might have done, but I hate it that you were facing all this alone. You need to remember you have friends who care about you and would do anything for you."

My eyes get misty.

Molly says, "That's right, Abby. And, as I started to say, I've found something that could possibly be useful." She's taken out her phone and is scrolling through images. "I mentioned that some of the documents Violet gave me recently go back, to the first generation of the Founders. Reading those, I came across this story that I never heard before ... Here it is."

She shows us her screen, a picture of a yellowed page with handwriting in black ink. "It seems that when the Founders first arrived here from the north, they encountered not only Lebab, but another spirit associated with the springs—an evil spirit. They called it a ca-thonic being."

"Cthonic," Ariel says. "It means 'from the Underworld'."

"Yeah, that's it. So the Founders tried several times to banish this creature, but it kept coming back. Finally, they devised this formulation where five of them went to the mouth of the springs. Four of them stationed at the four directions and one in the center. They used the chants recorded here to raise and direct the power of Lebab, and that was enough to banish that bad boy for good. What do you think?"

Well, my demon is based in St. Augustine just like this chthonic creature was based in Harmony Springs. But raising Lebab's energy in St. Augustine—or raising it here and sending it to St. Augustine? Both would probably prove ineffective. Still, there might be something in the ritual I could adapt ...

"Send me the file, and I'll look it over. Like you said, it might help. And thanks, Molly."

For the first time today, I see her smile.

〰〰

The furniture's been rearranged in the living room, clearing space along the four walls. Portraits of fountains symbolizing the Five Springs hang at different points. In front of each picture is a small table with a cup and a burning candle.

The room looks much like it did for my initiation rite, four years ago. The only difference is the people: Molly and Ariel weren't part of the Circle then, and Violet led the ceremony. Today, she is here only in spirit, the urn with her ashes set on a coffee table in the middle of the room. Today, Kevin leads the ritual. He stands in the doorway with a bowl of spring water. As each of us enters, he dips a finger in the bowl, traces a sign on our foreheads, a pentagram inside a circle, then touches the spot between the eyebrows, the third eye.

"Enter now. You are purified."

We gather at the center of the room. Kevin and Grandma wear their ceremonial robes. I'm dressed in a white gown that I wore at my initiation and at other ceremonies. Molly and Ariel are in street clothes, but barefoot, like the rest of us.

On the table, along with Violet's ashes, are her four magical tools. Kevin picks up the wand, a length of dark wood with a crystal bound at the tip. He uses it to trace a circle around the living room. Next, he picks up Violet's dagger and uses that to bind the circle. Holding both wand and dagger, he spreads his arms. We all face east as Kevin summons the Elementals of Air and asks them to bless our rite. We pivot with him as he repeats the invocation to the south for Fire, the west for Water, and finally the north for Earth.

"I now declare that the magical chamber is open."

Kevin sets down the tools, looks around at our faces and smiles. "Welcome dear friends on the path of true magic. Today we

-147-

remember and honor our companion on the path, Amor Verum, whose name in this earthly incarnation was Violet Morgan. In her honor, we will visit each of the Springs in symbolic fashion and review their lessons. As we do so, we will remember Violet and contemplate how her life exemplified each Principle of Harmony."

Kevin picks up a circular drum. He strikes it with his open hand as he leads the procession. We walk slowly, one step for each drumbeat. Reaching the first station, we gather before a portrait of a fountain, painted in shades of pale blue and rose.

"Behold you the Spring of the Love of Truth," Kevin says. "As true magicians, we give ourselves to the full power of this love, for it is the motive force for our magical work. The soul is a cauldron of will and desire, ever seething and bubbling. Only by binding your desires to the love of truth can you nourish your magic and your life."

He picks up a crystal goblet, takes a sip, then hands it to Grandma. "Remember our dear friend."

Each of us receives the cup and drinks. For a while, we stare at the portrait of the First Spring. I relax and my vision turns hazy. Violet's magical name, Amor Verum, means "love of truth." I think about all the truths she taught me—the hidden truths of Nature, how truth is often complex and multifaceted, how to discover the truth for myself by analyzing with the mind and then listening to the heart.

The procession moves on to the other Fountains, Endurance, Balance, Amity. By the time we stand before the Fountain of Bliss, I feel Violet's presence strongly—not like a ghost at my shoulder, but inside me—all her love and energy warming my heart.

I hope it will always be there.

♒

One last part of the funeral rite remains.

After we close the circle and put away the incense and candles, we change clothes and put on our shoes. Then, with Kevin carrying the urn, we go out the front door and march up the road to the top of

Bliss Spring. Turning off the road, we follow a path through the woods to a ceremonial circle that was laid out in the days of the Founders, and is always kept cleared. From the edge of the circle, we descend another path bordered with rocks, to a spot at the very top of the spring. We stand side-by-side overlooking the clear water.

Kevin speaks the ritual words: "Our beloved friend has resumed her journey on the inner planes, in the outer spheres. Her appearance has vanished from this time and place, but her presence abides with us and in the presence of All. Always, her mind and heart and soul will be with us, within the spirit of harmony."

With that, he empties the urn into Bliss Spring. We watch silently as Violet's ashes spread out in the water and flow away with the current.

〰

Back at the house we share a meal—mostly leftovers from the dinner last night. The mood is quiet but not gloomy. Around the dining room table, we share stories and reminiscences.

Kevin tells how he first met Violet. When he was a young man, his friend George Renshaw, my grandfather, invited him to visit Harmony Springs. Violet was leading the Circle of Harmony then, practicing with a few other people, most of them elderly. Kevin, already interested in spiritualism and magic, was fascinated. He and George decided to initiate. Later, Grandma fell in love with George, and she joined the circle too.

Molly talks a lot about all the books and papers Violet left her to read and analyze and how she now hopes to produce a "comprehensive" three- or four- volume history of the Circle.

Ariel is mostly quiet. Drawn out by Kevin's questions, he talks a little about his work in Orlando. Then he describes how he came to Harmony Springs and joined the circle because he "had seen the magic Abby could do."

"Violet was wonderful to me," he adds, looking at Kevin and Grandma. "You all were. I only regret that I haven't visited as often as I should. I let my studies lapse, distracted by too many other ambitions."

"Don't feel bad about that," Kevin tells him. "Distractions from the path have always been an issue, but even more so in the world we live in today. And this part has also always been true: every magician must find their own way."

Molly and I exchange a look. We can both relate to that.

"But as far as devoting yourself to magic," Kevin says, "I've got something that might give you some new impetus. I'll give it to you before you leave."

It turns out Kevin has gifts for all of us. After lunch, when Ariel is ready to drive home and Molly to head into town for a work shift, Kevin gathers us in the living room. To my surprise, he gives Molly Violet's wand and Ariel her dagger. He emphasizes that these gifts are tokens. If they choose to make them into their own magical tools, they will still need to consecrate them, after the proper advancement rites.

To Grandma, he gives Violet's cup, to symbolize the love Violet had for her. I wonder if he's going to give me Violet's other magical tool, the seeing stone, but again he surprises. From an old briefcase he takes a large book with worn leather covers and brass bindings. I've seen this book before.

"Her copy of the *Book of Lebab*," Kevin tells me. "I think she would want you to have it, Abby."

I've never owned a physical copy of the book, only the electronic one I've scanned. Now Violet has bequeathed me her own actual copy. As I thank Kevin, I have the feeling she's also bequeathed me a whole lot more.

That night, lying in bed after performing the Ablution Ritual, I open the book.

On the first page, below the title, I read:
Welcome, good friend on the Path of True Magic.
Herein you will find the Formulae of Magic revealed by LEBAB.
Use it only in accord with the Five Principles, lest your mind be
baffled and your soul lost in Great Confusion.

I spend way too long looking at the book. It was just last week that I searched through my electronic copy and found the formula I used to summon Inanna's power. That worked well enough. I came out of it charged with magical energy. And when I took that power into the game, I was able to defeat the demon with Inanna's fiery sigils. Of course, I did end up with a cut on my wrist requiring four stitches.

Call it a modest victory, or maybe a draw.

I still need something to vanquish Alyas for good and all.

Each formula in the book follows a basic pattern: call upon the aid of spirits, declare your intentions, raise energy—usually with a chant—and then release the power. I find a few examples that might be useful against Alyas, but it's hard to be sure. And, of course, there is the problem of how strong the magic taught by Lebab will be in St. Augustine, so far from the actual springs.

At last, deciding I'm just wandering in mental confusion, I close the book and go to sleep.

≈

The dream is luminous with the crystal blue light of the springs. I'm walking through deep woods, following a trail that curves and zigzags, similar to the path we walked to pour out Violet's ashes.

A spring seems to be somewhere ahead. I can hear the flowing water, but not see it. When I emerge into a clearing, I realize that the light and sound are not coming from a spring, but from a giant figure made of falling water.

Lebab.

The True Spirit of the Springs. His power is immense and old. His appearance is tall and ephemeral, long thin arms and legs, long flowing face and hair—all formed of clear water. He has no eyes, only empty spaces. Yet I know he is staring at me.

"Welcome, Fighting Eagle, initiate of the path."

I don't answer, just bow my head.

"We have spoken before," he tells me. "Now your spirit has called to me, through the book."

I can see how, subconsciously, I might easily have done that. "Yes, I ... Once again, I am haunted by an evil spirit, a demon this time. Not here, but in another place."

His eyeless face examines me. I feel him reading my soul. "Yes, an evil one of the underworld, very old. His power has grown strong, fed by humans. But any spirit enlivened by humans can also be diminished. Drain his power, and he will fade."

"That's what I've been trying to do. But, so far, he's been more than a match for me."

"Yes, I see you have allowed your magic to fade through disuse. But it is growing strong again. I will enliven you with all the power I can."

"Thank you."

"There is something else." Lebab looks down. The water flowing from his body has spread around his feet, so that now we stand in a shallow, shining pool. "One is needed to serve as Guardian of the Springs. This role has been mentioned to you before, I believe."

Yes, it has. Annie Renshaw first spoke of it that summer, four years ago. At the time, I felt inspired by the idea. In fact, it sparked my ambition to go into environmental law, because I wanted to be able defend the springs—and other natural places in Florida—in a practical, real-world way.

But ..."I've never learned exactly what it means. What would I have to do?"

"Focus the power of the Springs in your world, when called upon," Lebab answers. "Also, protect the Springs in their natural manifestation on the earth. The one who led the Circle of Harmony has now passed on. This makes the need for a true Guardian even more urgent. You are the rightful heir to this role. But you must be willing to accept the duty."

Well, I certainly want to protect the springs, and I want to honor Violet's legacy, and that of all the other true magicians. But there are already so many pressures on me, ambitions and distractions, as Ariel and Kevin were saying. And suppose I leave Florida to go to law school in the north ...?

"I want to help. But I'm just not sure."

The Spirit of the Springs stares at me a long moment. "Your decision can wait—but not for too long. Without a focus, the magic of the Springs will once again fade from your world."

"I understand." If I could just banish this demon and get my law school plans on track ...

"As was done in elder times, take one circuit of the planet around the star to decide. This was called 'a year and a day.' Use that time to learn the true desires of your soul, to cultivate your vision and your power. Return to me then with your decision."

I bow my head again. "Yes. Thank you."

"Hold out your wand."

I had not realized I had the wand, but there it is in my hand. I reach up and touch it to Lebab's extended fingertips. Power in the form of cool water pours down through the wood and into my body.

21. Time to play the game again

"Sweetie, you feel charged with energy this morning!"

Grandma and I are sharing breakfast in the warm, bright kitchen. While I was upstairs packing my bags, she fixed eggs and orange juice, toast and jam, and coffee of course.

"I think so, Grandma."

I slept hard and deep after my dream-conference with Lebab. Waking up, I felt the power of the Springs flowing in me. But also a kind of grim determination—to head back to St. Augustine and take care of business.

"And you feel okay about leaving?"

I gaze out past the open screen door to the green world. "Well, I'm never happy leaving you, Grandma. And I love Harmony Springs more than any place in the world. And, inside, I am grieving about Violet, of course. But with all that, yes, I feel okay."

She's quiet for a time, picking at her food while I eat.

"Are *you* okay, Grandma?"

She sets down her fork. "You know, I was all set this morning to urge you again to stay here. But now I've changed my mind. I think that might just have been selfishness, because I want you here with me. And I want you safe. But I understand why you have to leave."

I put down my fork and touch her wrist. "Right. I have work to do. And I have a demon to banish. Not sure how I'm going to do that yet, but I have to try."

Grandma considers. "Would you like me to come with you and stay for a while? I could find a room nearby. That way, you won't be so alone."

She's made that offer before. Tempting though it might be to have her close, to not feel so lonely, I have to refuse again, and for the same reason. If she were in St. Augustine, she would also be close to the demon—and vulnerable to his attack. That's a deal breaker.

"Thank you, Granma. I really appreciate the offer. But it doesn't feel like the right thing."

"Even for a little while?"

"Even for a little while." I get up from my chair and hug her shoulders. "I want you to promise to take care of yourself, okay? And I'll try to call more often, I promise."

Grandma laughs. "I can do the text thing too, you know? I've figured it out."

I leave a short time later. As I drive the county roads, I sense the magical energy of the Springs fading behind me—as if I'm traveling away from a beautiful sunset, heading into the night.

∿
∿

Just before noon, I park Veronica at the side of the house and carry my bags up the outside stairs. Cautiously, I open the door. Peeking inside, I scan the apartment, searching for weird shadows in the corners, sensing the air for evil emanations.

Nothing.

Good.

During the drive home, I thought about different magical operations I had read in the *Book of Lebab*, searching for anything that might help me get rid of Alyas for good. I also heard my phone click with an incoming text. Now, as soon as I set down my luggage, I check it.

Text from Molly. She's sent me a copy of the ceremony she mentioned, the one used by some of the Founders to banish the evil spirit that lived by the springs. She also sent a bunch of other pages with stuff she thought might be helpful.

So, after I take a shower and fix some tea, I sit down with my phone. The ceremony from the Founders is interesting. Five magicians got together and raised the power of Lebab. They stood in the woods near the mouth of the Springs and called him using a combination of chants and diagrams on paper. The drawings look like sigils, only here they are called "Figurations of Mental Power."

As I'm staring at my screen the room darkens. A sudden dread seizes my stomach. I twist around in the chair.

Alyas is standing behind me. "Time to play the game again."

I knock over the chair as I jump to my feet. I stagger backward, away from the demon. My magical tools are still in the suitcase, next to the door. I rush over there, kneel down and open it. My hands grope inside while my eyes stay fixed on Alyas.

He stands by the overturned chair, smiling, white teeth and red eyes in the broad, brown-orange face.

When I find the wand and dagger I stand. Holding them in front of me, I take a step toward him. "I'm not playing your stupid game anymore!"

His grin widens. "Oh, but you're wrong."

The clawed hands fly up, arms spread wide. Waves of power wash across the dim room, penetrating my skull, blinding me. Dizzy, I feel the wand and dagger fall from my hands. My body pitches forward, my arms and then my forehead smacking the floor.

〰〰

Alyas, Demon of the Ancient City.
Level 5

The title swims before my eyes in flaming letters.
How did I get here?
How did the demon suck me into the game so easily? With all the protections I've cast, I thought I was safe in my apartment. With the

power Lebab poured into me last night, I should have been even stronger.

Was all of that a delusion?

Fiery text flows over a screen of gray cloud:

> 1890. The Gilded Age. St. Augustine has become a vacation haven for wealthy northerners. In a luxury hotel room, John Newcombe of Boston ponders his fate. He has lost his family's fortune on risky investments. On the desk before him sits a bottle of an opiate called laudanum. A few drops will ease his physical pain. Drinking the whole bottle will end his pain forever.
> Alyas hovers nearby, savoring the man's misery and despair, urging him to drink.
> Your mission is to banish the demon or otherwise prevent the suicide.

My brain struggles to take in the story. I'm terrified. Over and over, I thought I'd gained sufficient power to banish the demon. Each time, he's come back stronger.

Over and over, I've failed.

The clouds disperse. I see a hotel room, elegantly furnished with oriental rugs and flowery wall-paper. Dizzy, I glance down at the wand and dagger, which have appeared in my hand.

I'm going to fail again. I squeeze that thought out of my brain.

A man—John Newcombe—sits in a gold-painted chair in front of an ebony desk. He wears a silk robe, pajamas, slippers. Black hair is slicked down, parted in the middle. A hand cups his chin, elbow propped on the desk. His expression is dull and lost.

Alyas looms behind the man, leans and whispers in his ear. "Drink, my friend, and all your troubles will be over."

The medicine bottle sits on the desk. Hesitantly, the man reaches for it.

I have to act. Raising the wand and dagger, I step toward the demon.

"Stop!"

John Newcombe freezes.

Alyas grins at me. "Ah, COH Girl has returned. You kept me waiting ..."

My brain is still hazy. I need to use the sigils of Inanna, but I can barely remember them. Instead, I draw a pentagram.

"Alyas, I banish you and cast you out."

The flaming star hovers in the air, then flickers out. The demon watches me, amused and undisturbed.

Newcombe's hand moves, fingers wrapping around the bottle.

Sigils! Squinting, I visualize the one called the *Might of Inanna*, a zigzag line like a lightning bolt. I use the dagger to draw it in the air.

"I banish you, Alyas. You cannot resist the might of the goddess!"

The sigil flows toward the demon—and disappears. Alyas laughs.

Did I draw the figure wrong, the lines in the wrong places?

Dread grips me as I start again. But my hand falters, shaking, My legs give out, and I collapse to my knees.

Alyas stands over me, arms spread wide. My body shudders, energy surging out of me, flowing up into the demon.

"Oh, yes!" he hisses. "So much magic power! Far too much for a single human to balance. But I—I can absorb it all!"

I collapse onto the rug, lying on my side, literally drained.

Alyas points to the man at the desk. John Newcombe raises the bottle to his mouth and swallows the liquid down.

"Yes!" Alyas cries, full of joy.

The man slumps in his chair, staring glassy-eyed. His arms sink, and the bottle drops onto the rug.

"Wonderful. Wonderful!" Alyas laughs.

The scene vanishes, covered now with flowing black smoke. A harsh buzzing sounds in my ears as orange letters flash:

> You have failed at Level 5.
> Game Over.

♒

Waking up. Fuzzy vision comes into focus—the floor of my apartment.

Stinking breath, a whisper in my ear. "Wake up, Abby Renshaw. You have lost the game."

"Eek!" I roll over and scramble away from the demon, crawling backwards until my shoulders touch the wall.

Alyas crouches down and looks me in the eye, smirking. My wand and dagger lie on the floor behind him. I need to stand up and order him away.

But I feel so weak, dizzy, my head swimming.

He sneers. "The weakness will only get worse, you see? All those times you thought you were banishing me, it was *I* absorbing *your* power. This last time though, this was the best." He puts three fingers together and kisses the clawed tips. "Delicious."

I shake my head in disbelief.

"Oh, it's true! Did you really believe I would allow my presence to be absorbed in a fabricated game? No! I was playing with you. You and that foolish man Jeremy, who fancies himself a wizard. But now the game is over."

I stare at him stupidly. He leans in close, his breath brushing my cheek.

"You will never banish me again. I shall be with you whenever I choose. You and Jeremy both. You will be seeing much more of me from now on."

His horrible laugh makes me whimper.

"You see? I told you once how I feed on moments of despair. So I have led you here, step by step. Now, I will visit you again and again, until I have exhausted all of your misery. Then, and only then, I will let you put an end to it."

I squeeze my eyes shut, groaning.

"You know what I mean, of course? Yes! The only way you will end it is to make an end to yourself. You saw how much I enjoyed the suicide of that fool Newcombe. Perhaps you will be next ...?"

"No! I won't!"

"I've already made you cut your wrist once. Perhaps deeper next time? Or will you decide to jump off the Bridge of Lions? The top of the Lighthouse? I think I shall make this our new game: Who will die first: you? Jeremy? Or that foolish girl called Canary? Of course, there will be others. With the power I have gained from you, there will be no end to my enjoyment in this time ..."

"No ..." Moaning low in my throat. This is a nightmare, and I desperately need to wake up. My head rolls back against the wall.

22. You appear to be trapped in the Great Below

Sinking down and down in gray water. No light in any direction.

Long ago, I had recurring nightmares of drowning in Bliss Bayou. But I'm not drowning now. I don't need to breathe. I'm a disembodied spirit. My life is over. It all happened long ago.

Have I already killed myself? My mind tells me the water is the Matanzas River. Did I jump off the Bridge of Lions after all?

Matanzas, the place of slaughter. All the world is slaughter. All of history is cruelty and death.

Hopeless. I've seen too much of it, playing the demon game. There is nothing more I can do. How stupid I was to think I could make a difference, fight the evil. The demon was playing me all along, using me, stealing my magic.

Now, it's all gone ...

〰

Opening my eyes, I search through the darkness in confusion.

Eventually, I realize I'm in my apartment, still sitting on the floor. Faint twilight gleams at the window curtains. Hours must have passed.

So weak. Still dizzy.

I stand up, lurch two steps, stumble to the floor. On hands and knees, I crawl across the carpet. It takes all my strength to hoist myself onto the bed.

Slipping into the dark again ...

Scenes come and go—visions or nightmares? I can't tell the difference. The massacre of the French prisoners on the shore of the inlet. An infirmary where children are dying of the yellow fever. Prisoners tortured at the Old Jail. Me, lying in a hospital bed while my hands and feet are amputated. I feel it all—slicing pain, burning fever, choking on my own blood.

Agony. I have to make it stop ...

Daylight. I'm standing in the kitchen. A drawer is open, a carving knife in my hand. I slide the blade gently over my wrist ...

"No!" Realizing what this is, I drop the knife. It clatters on the floor.

Dizzy again. I clutch my scalp with both hands.

Have to find my phone. Call for help ... Grandma or Molly ...

Glancing around, I spot the phone on my work table. I stumble toward it, lose balance, end up on my hands and knees.

I struggle to rise. But my arms give out and my forehead thumps on the carpet. As my mind slides away again, I hear Alyas' mocking voice.

"You are not alone, Abby Renshaw. I am here with you."

♒

All the torment of the world is a bottomless, slow moving river—black, mucky water streaked with green sludge. Sweeping my arms, kicking my feet, struggling to stay afloat. Otherwise, I will sink and die.

I won't give up. I'm a fighter. I've always been a fighter.

Except now, I'm at the end of my strength. The foundations of my life have dissolved. I need help. But who can help me? Violet is gone. Grandma and Kevin, Molly and Ariel are all far away. Lebab and my spirit guides are distant or else blocked from me.

"Inanna!" As I'm about to sink, I call her name, screaming like a desperate child.

"Do not leave me here, Goddess. Do not abandon me!"

I thrash the water, scream her name over and over, calling from the depths of my heart because there is nothing else I can do. "I would be your priestess and use your power for good in the world. Save me, Goddess. Please save me."

For an instant, I sense her presence—a flickering of cloudy light, a brush of wings.

"Inanna, I call you!"

The presence brightens to a dazzling glow. I am lifted up. Wings of light have sprouted on my back. I rise above the water.

Inanna appears in a golden hallow. Her piercing eyes gaze at me. It is her eyes that are holding me up. Looking down, I see the Bridge of Lions, the Matanzas River, no longer dark and sluggish, but blue and sparkling in the sunlight. Off to the north, I can see all the way to where it flows into the ocean.

<p style="text-align:center">~~~</p>

A single candle glows. The light flickers on walls painted with murals. I'm seated in a heavy chair, like a throne, dressed in a long skirt, fringed shawl, gold jewelry—like the priestesses of Inanna wore in ancient times. But when I try to stand, my arms and legs won't move. I am chained at the wrists and ankles.

"It appears you are trapped in the Great Below, my priestess. Even as once I was." Inanna floats in front of a bolted iron door.

"How can I escape from here?"

She pauses a moment, considering. "I shall send spirits to try to free you. That is how I was freed."

She moves away, vanishes through the locked door.

The candle goes out. I sit alone, chained in the dark.

How much time passes? I don't know. I just keep thinking how scared I am—and how tired.

I just want it all to end. I think about being back in my physical body, in the kitchen, holding the sharp knife at my wrist.

No! I won't do that. Not ever. I've always been a fighter, and I'm still a fighter.

The door swings open on creaking hinges, flooding the room with gray light from outside. My whole body stiffens with panic. *Has the demon come again?*

A tiny winged creature loops into the room. I can just see it in the slanting light—a dragonfly or ... hummingbird. It hovers near me, blue wings and ruby-feathered head.

When it speaks, it has the voice of that other Hummingbird, Canary's sister.

"Come on, Abby," she urges me. "It's time to go!"

"I can't go. I'm chained here."

"No, you're not!"

The moment she says that, I feel a pop. My arms lift up, my feet shift.

Climbing out of the chair, I see the chains are gone. And now I'm dressed in my regular clothes—T-shirt, shorts, running shoes.

"Come on, Abby. Hurry!"

Hummingbird swoops from the room. I dash after her.

We enter a long corridor, lit along the way with lamps. The plain stone walls remind me of the coquina rock at the Spanish fort. Hummingbird flies ahead, stopping sometimes to look back and call for me to hurry.

I'm running as hard as I can, but the passageway seems endless. Soon, I'm panting, struggling to keep up. The bird keeps getting farther ahead. The thought occurs that I shouldn't have let my conditioning lapse.

Finally, Hummingbird comes to the end of the tunnel, a wall of yellow light. She pauses one more time to be sure I'm following, then darts through the barrier.

When I reach the light, I stop to catch my breath, then step through.

I've crossed into another realm. A full moon shines in a starry, pale-blue sky. I stand on wet grass, at the edge of a clearing surrounded by trees and shrubbery, caressed by cool gentle air.

I know this place: the circle at the top of Bliss Spring.

Somehow it seems different, the foliage not as tall or thick, the grass softer. And the stones set up at the center to form an altar—they look newer, not so worn.

As I stare at the altar, a figure fades into view. A young woman, dressed in a silver and white robe. Reddish brown hair falls past her shoulders. She wears a wreath of white flowers like a crown. She does not notice me, just gazes down through the woods in the direction of the water. Her palms rest flat on the altar stone.

There's a reason I'm here, so I'd better find out what it is.

I step toward the altar. A few yards away, I stop and clear my throat to announce my presence. The woman looks at me, smiles, and in that smile I know her.

"Violet." The young Violet, or rather her spirit, when she was in her twenties and first joined the Circle of Harmony.

"There you are, Abby dear. It's so good to see you."

I step closer. "You knew I was coming?"

That joyful smile again. "I was told to expect you."

She reaches her hands out in welcome. As I touch them, I envision gold angel wings sprouting on her back.

Violet grins. In her eyes and in her touch, I feel tremendous energy. This is magic I've felt before, but seldom this strong or whole—peaceful, harmonious, unfailing. The power of the Springs.

It brings tears to my eyes. As I blink them away, the scene changes again.

We sit in Violet's kitchen. Teacups and saucers on the table, bright daylight behind the windows and screen door. Violet is older now, in her sixties perhaps. But not in decline as she's been the past few years, still robust and full of life.

Still beaming at me. "How are you, dear?"

I wipe away another tear. "Much better now that I'm with you. But ... Not sure what I'll do next. I mean, back there in the physical world."

Violet nods, pressing her lips. "Perhaps a reading?"

She hold up a deck of tarot cards.

"Yes, please."

I shuffle the cards and hand them back. She lays them out in a line. I see now that, in whatever realm we're currently inhabiting, the cards have lives of their own. Not only do the images move, but as I examine each card I am drawn into the scene. Dreamlike, I hear Violet's voice discussing each card that I visit.

"*The Fool*. A significant card. Stepping out of the higher realms into the physical world. I suppose that is you, Abby. Starting your new life in St. Augustine."

The next card is the *Ten of Wands*, a man struggling to carry a heavy burden. "This journey has not been easy. But true growth seldom is ..."

That image fades and I stand before a massive throne, a huge, gruesome creature seated there. "*The Devil*," Violet says. "A terrible adversary who has blocked your way, forced you to alter your journey."

Just as my fear of the demon rises, he fades, and I move into the next card. A man lies on his belly, likely dead, swords stuck in his bleeding body.

"*Ten of Swords*," Violet comments. "You have come to a place of utter defeat. But this is not the end of the reading."

In the next card, I see myself, standing tall, holding a sword in both hands, a fierce expression on my face. "*Page of Swords*. You are ready to fight once more."

I admire how tough the Page looks, and wonder where I can find such confidence again.

Then I shift into the next card. Five guys are fighting with clashing sticks. "The *Five of Wands*," Violet's voice declares. "A battle is forecast. You join with others against your adversary."

The clamor fades into another scene. Three women dance in celebration, holding three goblets high. "Oh, that is very good," Violet says. "The *Three of Cups* foretells victory and celebration."

Back in her kitchen, I lift my eyes from the last card in the line. "That *is* very good. But I've no idea how to get there."

"Hmm." Violet touches her lip, then points her finger at the *Page of Swords*, me rising to fight again. "I think that up till now, Abby, you have tried to carry the fight alone. It has proven too much for you." Her fingertip moves to the next card, the *Five of Wands*. "It is okay to call on others for help."

That feels right. I sure could use some help against this demon. But who, and how?

I imagine myself in a circle with other magicians, casting a formulation that would defeat Alyas for good. That reminds me of the paper Molly sent me, the account of the ceremony several of the Founders used to banish the evil spirit from the springs.

"Yes, I remember that one." Violet has read my mind. "Four magicians at the cardinal points, one in the center. Of course, the Founders tapped into the power of Lebab, here at the Springs. That won't be very strong in St. Augustine, where you must work ... But then, you have another spirit you can call on."

"You mean Inanna?"

"That's right, dear. The one who sent me to you." Violet stands. "Yes. I think that formulation from the Founders might just do the trick—with some adaptations of course. But you've always been good at that, Abby."

I stand up too, scratch my head, smile. "Yeah. I guess so."

"Just remember." Violet points to her heart. "Do your best work, then let go of the results. You know that principle."

"The final key to Bliss." I learned that lesson early on the magical path, the first time I had to banish an evil entity. In a vision, I had found my way to the last of the Springs, the Fountain of Bliss. The ghost of my grandfather, George Renshaw, appeared and told me how he had learned, in his life, that you can only do your best, then had to let go and, as he put it, "Let the Universe do its thing."

As I'm recalling this, the scene changes again. The Fountain of Bliss floats before me, a rounded, crystal waterfall, seemingly with no source and no basin.

Violet is still with me, the young version again, standing in front of the Fountain. With her is someone else, a young man with long hair and a beard, wearing jeans and a sort of cowboy hat—the ghost of my grandfather, George Renshaw.

"Hey there, Fighting Eagle." He grins and takes hold of Violet's hand. In life, I know, they were good friends. "I'm glad you remember that lesson about Bliss. Now go and get that demon." He lifts Violet's hand. "We'll all be rooting for you."

Both of them beam at me, their forms growing brighter. Once again, I feel that tremendous current of magic pouring into me—the peaceful, bottomless power of the Springs.

"Goodbye, dear," Violet calls. "Do stay in touch."

"I will. I promise."

Gratefully, I soak in the magic. After a while, the spirits fade, leaving me alone with the Fountain of Bliss.

23. The owl was very insistent

Loud knocking draws me slowly out of the deep, deep trance. A woman's voice is calling.

"Abby! Hey, Abby. Are you in there?"

Reality flows into my brain. I'm lying on the carpet in the center of my apartment, daylight at the windows, persistent pounding on the door. Climbing to my knees, I look over the room. No lurking demons, no spirits of any kind.

"Abby? Are you okay?"

I stand and stagger to the door. The voice sounds familiar. But you have to be careful.

"Who is it?"

"Cary Greene."

That's who it sounds like. Leaving the chain lock on, I open the door a crack. She peers at me from the landing.

"Are you all right?" she asks.

"What are you doing here?"

"I had to come. The owl was very insistent."

That has to be Canary. I shut the door, take off the lock, open it and motion her in. As soon as she crosses the threshold, I close and lock the door again.

Squinting, I repeat her words. "The owl was insistent ... ?"

"Yeah." She tosses up both hands. "I mean, last night, I was asleep at my mom's place. In the middle of the night, I hear this owl hooting outside the window. It keeps it up and keeps it up, and finally I get out of bed and ask her what she wants. She said you were in trouble, and I had to go and help you—like right away."

I'm thinking: Another spirit sent by Inanna?

"I was reluctant, to be honest," Canary says. "I mean, we'd already sent you protection, the three of us, and I asked her what more she thought I could do alone. And the owl said, 'magic,' and if I ever wanted to respect myself again, I better get moving and get here today."

"Today...?" I look around for my phone, wondering what time it is—and what day, for that matter.

"What day is it?"

"Monday. Monday afternoon."

"Oh ..."

So, I've been in the Great Below about twenty-four hours. And I missed work today. Sheldon and Bond won't be pleased, not at all. Can't worry about that now. I'm just trying to piece together this moment.

"So, you drove here, from Lake Sylvan?"

"Yes. I had to borrow my mom's car. She wasn't happy about it. But Hummingbird was even more insistent than the owl. She wanted to come too. Mom drew the line there. She allowed me to take the car, but not my little sister. Hummingbird said to tell you she'd be here in spirit."

I flash back to the hummingbird flying into the dungeon cell, freeing me from my chains. "I know that already ... I think."

"Are you feeling okay?

"Yeah ..." I pause to examine that question. The power of Bliss Spring beats strongly in my veins. "Good, actually. Very good."

Canary looks perplexed. "So, was my coming here all a wild goose chase then?"

"No!" I touch the top of her arm. "I do need your help. If you're willing."

She pulls back her shoulders. "I'm willing."

"Even if it means doing magic?

"Yes. I know the demon is still around and, after what you've done for me ... I mean, I still wish my life was not so weird, but if I have to use magic to protect myself—and my friends—I'll do what I have to do."

I smile and tilt my head. "Come on in."

My mind is racing. The ceremony the Founders used to banish the chthonic spirit, the one Molly sent me: Violet thought that would do nicely. It calls for five practitioners. Canary and I make two. Molly will want to be in on it, and I know I can count on Ariel. Not sure where to find number five though. But I can probably adapt the ritual to work with four. Like Violet said, I've always been good at adapting.

I gesture Canary to the sofa. "Would you like some coffee or breakfast?"

She laughs. "Breakfast? At four in the afternoon?"

"Is it that late?" I'm still pulling reality back together. Journeys to the Great Below can be so confusing. "By the way, how did you find my apartment?" She hasn't been here before, and I don't think I gave her the address.

"You told me you lived in this neighborhood. I drove around until I spotted your car." She sits up straight, looking worried. "That reminds me: I saw a guy parked outside in a red MINI Cooper. He seemed to be watching the house. Gave me the creeps."

"Oh, really?" *Jeremy.* Why is *he* here?

"I sensed he's somehow connected to the demon."

"He is."

For just a second, I wonder what to do. Then I march over to my work table and pick up my dagger and wand.

"Think I'll go have a word."

Canary follows me to the door. "Really? You think you should?"

"Yeah. He's creepy for sure, but I can handle him."

We march down the steps and up the shell driveway. When we approach Jeremy's car, the door swings open. He climbs out awkwardly. Seeing the wand and dagger, he raises two empty hands.

"Don't get excited. I just want to talk."

I pull up, glaring at him, Canary standing at my shoulder. He's glances at her, surprised, I think, to see us together.

"Talk then," I tell him. "We're listening."

"Well, uh, I know you lost the last round of the game. But it isn't necessarily over. I've got ideas for other scenarios. You could maybe keep playing, and we'll refine ..."

"Not interested. Go away."

"But—"

"Why are you really here?"

His arms flop down. "The demon. He said with the game over, he doesn't need me anymore. But he won't leave me alone. He's trying to make me jump out the window, or crash my car ... I took a big risk just driving over here. You've got to help me."

Well, I did try to warn him that Alyas was using him. But at this point, I-told-you-sos are pointless. Jeremy sounds so desperate. This time I do feel sorry for him.

"Listen. Here's my advice: Go home. Shut down all your devices, lock yourself in. And if you think you might actually kill yourself, call a suicide prevention hotline."

"That's it?" he yells. "But what about the demon?"

"I'm working on that. Now get out of here—And *don't* come back."

He gapes at me, helpless, for a few seconds. Then, resigned, he climbs into his car and starts up the engine.

I wait for him to drive away before heading back inside.

"That was weird," Canary says. "When he started talking, I sort of remembered him from my demon nightmares. He was the guy in the wizard's robe, right?"

"Right."

"What's this about a game?"

"Long story."

I'm wondering how much to explain about the game as we climb the stairs. But as soon as we step inside, we both let out a yelp. The place is unnaturally dark—except for the orange glow of the demon floating in the middle of the room.

Breath hisses between my teeth. I'm terrified. If anything, Alyas seems bigger and more powerful than ever.

"Hello, Abby Renshaw." He smiles. "You ought to have been nicer to poor Jeremy, you know. Can't you save him from the big, bad demon?"

Fighting to appear calm, I hold the wand and dagger crossed in front of me. "We'll see."

The demon laughs. "Oh, but you are feisty. And, I must say, surprising. I thought your spirit obliterated, and yet here I find you just one day later, romping around with the witch girl and threatening me again with your magic."

He's appears amused, but behind that there just might be a shade of doubt. I've probably surprised him, coming back so soon and so strong. That thought gives me hope.

I trace a sigil of Inanna with the wand. It sparkles in the air. "This time I think we'll play a different game," I suggest. "But instead of Jeremy, I'll be the one setting up the story."

Alyas stares at the figure of blue fire. "Really? And why should I agree to that, instead of just destroying you?"

Behind the sigil, I use the dagger to trace a banishing pentagram. "Because, to destroy me, you'd have to take over my mind. Not so easy, as I think you've learned. But this new game might give you the chance. Who knows?"

Pointing the wand and dagger, I send the two fiery figures flowing toward him. "But for now, you have to leave. I'll call you when the game is ready."

Alyas raises a hand, halting the sigil and pentagram in mid-air. His laugh sounds hollow. "Well, how can I refuse such an intriguing invitation? Very well, I will go for now. But I will leave you both something to remember me by."

His long arm sweeps the air, pushing the fiery images back across the room. As the demon vanishes, the two shapes accelerate. I lean aside as they pass over my shoulder.

Behind me, Canary screams."Ow! Oh! Owwww!"

In a blaze of heat, I pivot to face her. Her hands are clapping her scalp. Her long yellow hair has burst into flames.

This must be an illusion. But I can't take the chance.

Dropping the wand and dagger, I grip her arm and yank her into the kitchen. Canary's still screaming as I flip on the faucet and thrust her head into the sink, her face pushing aside an unwashed cup and saucer. Flames sizzle and smoke as the water gushes, drenching her head.

In a moment, the fire and smoke are all gone.

Canary stands up and gazes at me, baffled. "What? Oh ..." She checks her dripping head with both hands. "Not real?"

"Apparently. Sorry about the dirty dishes."

"Oof." She wipes her forehead. "Thank god I still have my hair."

〰

Head damp, a towel draping her shoulders, Canary sits at the kitchen table with a cup of coffee. In the other chair, I devour yogurt and cereal, and talk between mouthfuls.

"Not a game, really. I just said that to the demon to put him off for now."

"So what *are* you planning?"

"Well, I have this ritual. It was composed long ago by members of the magical society that founded Harmony Springs. They used it to banish a chthonic spirit that dwelled near the springs."

"Ca-thonic?"

"Yeah. It means 'underworld.' Apparently, this guy was a bad one, like our demon. And, like our demon, his source of energy was a particular place on the earth."

"In our case, St. Augustine."

"Yup. And that's why the ritual needs to be done outdoors. I'm thinking the ground right at the base of the Bridge of Lions, because I believe our demon's connected to the Matanzas River."

"That's where I've mostly seen him." Canary shivers and glances around uneasily, making sure he hasn't come back.

I'm not worried about that. After he vanished, I did protective magic to banish him from the apartment for now. Three times, just to make sure.

"So, at the Bridge of Lions," Canary says. "What'll we do?"

"Well, this ritual is exceptionally powerful, for two reasons. One, it requires the focused intent of several magicians. They had five in the original version, but I'm thinking I can work it with four."

"Four ...?"

"Me and you, and a couple of my friends, who I'm hoping will help us out."

"Okay. What's the other reason it's so powerful?"

"The magicians stand in a circle and together they invoke the energy of an extremely powerful spirit. In the original case, they called on Lebab, the spirit of the Springs. In our case, we'll be calling on the Goddess Inanna. Do you know her?"

"Babylonian or something, right? Growing up a Wiccan, I've come across a lot of goddesses."

"Yes, Mesopotamian, known as the Queen of Heaven and Earth. I've invoked her power before. She helped me come back after the demon knocked me out this last time." *Was that really just one day ago?* "In the ritual, we'll invoke her power using sigils. Are you familiar with sigils?"

Canary shows an uncertain frown. "I've heard of them ..."

"They're like diagrams that encapsulate a spell or spiritual power. Don't worry. I'll show you what you'll need to do."

She takes a sip and then sets down her cup. "Okay. When do we do this goddess-invoking, demon-banishing sigil ritual?"

We both laugh at the way she's put it. I guess it is pretty convoluted, (story of my life.) "As soon as I can get the group together. Tomorrow, I hope."

"Oh, tomorrow would be good. August 1st, you know? That's Lammas, one of the eight Wiccan sabbats. Excellent for group magic."

〰

After finishing my late, late breakfast, I send a text to both Molly and Ariel: "I need your help. Please call when you get a chance."

Minutes later, as I'm teaching Canary a crash course in sigil magic, I hear back from Molly. "Abby! What you got for me?"

Briefly, I explain how things have come down to crunch time with the demon, and that I'm going to use the Founders ritual that she discovered.

"Cool." Molly says.

"I was hoping you'd be one of the circle. Are you willing?"

"Of course. When?"

"Can you get here early tomorrow? It has to be done in St. Augustine."

"Umm, yeah. I'll rearrange my work schedule. I'll tell my boss something's come up. I can get there by around ten."

"That would be great, Molly. Thank you."

"The ritual calls for five all together, right? Who else have you got?"

"Well, there's me and Canary Greene, and I'm hoping to get Ariel up here."

"Oh, I'm sure he'll want to help. He's still crazy about you, you know?"

Not something I've been thinking about, but it gives me a warm little quiver.

"That's still only four," Molly says.

"I know. I figure I can adapt it to work with four. I'm also revising it to use the sigils of Inanna. Going to work on all that tonight."

"Oh." Molly might sound a shade doubtful. But she says: "Okay then. I'll see you around ten."

While we were talking, my phone showed another call coming in—from Ariel. As soon as Molly rings off, I call him back.

"Hi, Abby. Is everything okay?"

"Yeah, I'm good, but ... Listen, Ariel. I know this is a big ask, but you said I should call you if I needed help, and ... Could you possibly drive up here first thing tomorrow? There's this ritual ..."

"Is this about the demon?"

"Yeah. I'm going to try to ground him for good. But I'll need—"

"I'll be there."

That same warm quiver touches my heart. "Ariel, I can't tell you how grateful—"

"Don't worry about that. Just tell me what I'll need to do. For preparation."

I spend a few minutes explaining the Founders' ritual and how I'll be adapting it to use the sigils of Inanna. Ariel decides to do a ritual for Inanna this evening, on his own, to familiarize himself with her energy. That sounds like a good idea to me, and I promise to text him the images of the eight sigils, some or all of which we'll be using tomorrow.

When the call ends, I look across the table at Canary, who is watching me with an amused expression. "You know some interesting people," she observes.

∿∿

Next morning, I wake up dreading a lot of things. One of them, I have to do alone and right away. That is, calling the law office to apologize for being out all day yesterday. *And* for not responding to their call or texts. And, worse still, explain that I'm going to be out again today.

It's not like I had any choice about missing so much work these past weeks.

It's also not like I can give them the real reasons all this happened. At this point, I can't even think up a plausible excuse.

Not sure why I'm dreading the call so much. I've probably already blown any chance that they'll write me a decent recommendation for law school. Heck, they might just decide to dispense with my services right now.

Still, I have to call and try. Otherwise, it would be unprofessional. So, after sharing some extra strong coffee with my houseguest Canary, I punch the reply icon on my phone and ring up the office.

Gloria recognizes my number. "Abby, where have you been?"

"I'm really sorry, Gloria. I've been ill again."

"Do you need help?"

"No. I'm recovering now. I just need another day. I know I've missed a lot of time, but it just couldn't be helped. Please apologize for me to Teresa and Larry, and tell them I'll be in tomorrow and try to explain myself."

Yeah. Good luck with that.

But I *do* plan to go to work tomorrow, and I *will* have to come up with some way to plead my case ...

Assuming, of course, I survive today.

24. A circle at the Lion Bridge

The original rite was called *A Supernal Convocation to Cast Down the Chthonic Entity*. According to everything Molly was able to discover, it was performed only once, in 1886. This was in the earliest days of Harmony Springs as a spiritualist colony.

The colony was founded in 1882 by two men from the north, one from New York and one from Indiana. According to the story, both were visited in a dream on the same night by the spirit of Lebab, who told them to come to Florida and build a community. There was no town near the springs then, just a little backwoods settlement.

But this was the heyday of spiritualism in America, and the colony grew quickly. People camped out and slept in tents or wagons. Some were mediums who channeled spirits. Others practiced various forms of occultism and magic.

Before long, members of the community found their connection with Lebab interrupted by another being, one that haunted dreams, disrupted trance work, and actually frightened some of the colonists so much that they left. None of the papers give the name of this creature, but it's always identified as an "evil spirit" or "chthonic entity."

Occultists tried to exorcise the thing, but it kept coming back. Finally, the community leaders banded together to take action. They devised a ritual to raise the power of Lebab and focus it to banish the troublesome spirit. That ritual marked the start of the Circle of Harmony as a magical society.

Tuesday morning, while waiting for my friends to arrive, I study the nineteenth century rite and compare it to the revised version that I composed last night. Like many Circle of Harmony ceremonies, it began by casting a sphere of protection, then calling the Elemental spirits—Earth, Air, Fire, and Water. Four magicians stood in a circle, one at each of the cardinal points. Each of them held a glass picture frame on which was drawn a symbol, a combination of the name "Lebab" and a pentagram representing the direction—north, south, east, or west. The fifth person stood in the center, holding a wooden wand topped by a crystal. After stating their intention—to banish the underworld spirit—the group focused their minds on Lebab and chanted a verse to summon his energy. With his power raised, they recited a second chant to call the evil being and bind him in the circle. Then they directed Lebab's energy to drain away the creature's power. Several of the participants reported seeing him as a quivering shadow, which faded and faded and finally shrank into the earth.

For my version of the rite, I plan to summon Inanna's power. Instead of diagrams based on Lebab's name, we will focus on her sigils—handily displayed on our phones. There are eight sigils, and at first I thought to use them all. But then I was inspired to simplify and just use four, which happen to correspond to the four directions. As for the chants, I've written my own to summon both Inanna's power and then the demon. I'm no poet, but they are only a few verses, and I even managed to make them rhyme. The important thing about the chants is, again, to focus our minds on raising power.

Those are the only adaptations I've made. Except, of course, with just four of us instead of five, I'll need to serve as both the person in the center and at one of the quarters.

I hope all this will work. As I go over the details with Canary, sharing text and sigils on our phones, it sounds kind of weak.

"Is this making sense?" I ask with a slight grimace.

"Actually, it feels really powerful to me. Not my mother's magic, that's for sure."

"Is that good or bad?"

"In this case good. I do have a question though."

"Yes?"

"Well, four of us are going to stand in the park, at the base of the Bridge of Lions, and do this whole ritual, with chanting and sigils, in broad daylight. But there's likely to be tourists walking by, and definitely cars whizzing around, like ten yards away. Isn't it all going to be too ... public?"

I had thought about that, a little. "Well, I don't think we'll be *too* conspicuous. Mainly, four people standing around looking at their phones."

"But suppose someone walks up and interrupts us?"

I consider that. "You're right. We'll cast a formula of concealment before we head down there."

Canary frowns. "Seriously?"

"Yeah. There's one in the *Book of Lebab*. It won't literally make us invisible, just really hard to notice."

I open the book on my phone and scroll through to find the spell in question, *A Formulation to Conceal Public Magic*. I'm walking through it with Canary when I hear someone climbing the outside stairs. We're both on our feet when the knock comes.

"Abby. It's Ariel."

Grinning, I pull open the door and throw my arms around him. "Thank you so much for coming!" He feels solid and strong, and he smells like lemon aftershave.

"Of course." He laughs. "Thank you for the warm greeting."

A little embarrassed, I pull him inside and introduce him to Canary. They smile at each other, and I sense maybe a little spark of attraction between them. Or is that just me?

I give Ariel my chair at the table and pour him some coffee. "I hope it won't cause you trouble to miss work on such short notice."

"I called in sick," he shrugs. "Should not be a problem. I can make up the work tonight and tomorrow. Now tell me what we're going to do about this demon."

I text him the files, and the three of us sit at the table reviewing the steps of the ritual. Ariel studies the chants, asks questions on a few points. After talking it over, we assign Canary to the south, the element of Fire, and Ariel to the west and Water. Molly is very much an Air person, so we'll put her in the east. That leaves me to cover the north and Earth on the circle, as well as the center place. I will bring my wand and the appropriate sigil.

We're about to begin a walkthrough of the ritual when I hear more noise outside. This sounds like *two* people coming up the steps. Worried, I hurry over to the door and ask who it is.

"Molly."

Opening the door, I see not only my best girlfriend, but someone else from Harmony Springs—a slender Black man with glasses and short gray hair.

"Kevin!"

His smile is fond and sad. He lost his life partner only a week ago. "Hello, Abby."

Stepping outside, I give him a hug. "I can't believe you came."

"Listen," Molly says. "I just thought: this ritual was designed for five, we should have five. So I dropped over to see Kevin and told him the plan. He volunteered."

"Right," Kevin agrees. "Assuming an old professor can be of help, I'm your man. Seriously, when Molly told me what you planned to do, and that you were needing one more person, how could I not? Violet would want me to—the duty of a true magician."

My eyes grow moist. "I'm so grateful. Come on in."

After showing them over to the sofa, and dragging extra chairs from the kitchen area, I start a new pot of coffee. At my back, I hear them all conversing about their different magical backgrounds and experiences. Canary grew up in Wicca and has some exposure to other traditions. Kevin has many years working in the Circle of Harmony and, as an anthropologist, has studied cultures all over the world. Molly has read a lot about everything, and practiced a little with the Circle. Ariel too, is an initiate, but has also worked a lot with the free-form discipline called Postmodern Magic. Listening to their discussion, I feel my confidence growing—like a team of superheroes has come to my aid.

♒

Rehearsal.

We've pushed furniture out of the way and arranged ourselves in the middle of the apartment. We all have phones in hand, with my revised text and the appropriate sigils. Kevin's taken the station at the north, freeing me to stand in the center.

It's just past eleven. I figure we'll practice for an hour or so before heading down to the Bridge of Lions.

Noon on a day in high summer—sounds like a perfect time for banishing a demon.

We practice through the opening of the ritual, the casting of a protective sphere, the words I'll use to invoke the goddess, then to call and bind the demon. We drill ourselves on the chants and practice focusing on the sigils.

Something about that part feels not quite right.

With Kevin unexpectedly appearing to take the place at the north, I reconsidered what sigil I should place in the center. In addition to the ones associated with the four quarters, there are four other sigils of Inanna, representing her different powers. I choose the one called *Might of Inanna*, but staring at it now makes me woozy.

Dizziness washes into my brain. My knees go weak. Next thing I know, I'm down with my face on the carpet.

Then the *next* thing I know, I'm walking through a huge hall. Torches on square pillars cast firelight on ancient paintings. Ahead of me, the floor rises three steps to a platform. Inanna is seated on a throne, flanked by resting lions.

"Approach, my priestess."

I walk to the bottom of the steps and bow. Inanna rises and moves down the steps, the lions slinking quietly beside her. "You have done well," she says. "Now I can invest you with more power."

She holds a kind of wand, with two curved blades attached at the sides and twin lion heads at the top.

"The Mace of Rulership confers power to use in my name." She holds it out for me to take. "This power can help you vanquish any demon."

Mouth open in awe, I lift my hand. As I touch the silvery wood, energy flows up my arm to my heart. The mace pulses, flattening in form so that the blades become like crescent moons and the lion heads change into sunbursts.

"Abby? Abby, are you okay?"

Back in the apartment, on my knees, my four friends hovering over me.

"Uh, yeah."

Kevin and Ariel each grip an arm and help me to stand.

"How long was I out?"

"Just a minute," Kevin says.

"Well, this is not a promising start," Canary puts in.

"No. No, it's good," I answer. "Really good"

I rush over to the work table, grab a pen and paper. Quickly, I draw the image: a rod in the center, two crescent moons, two sunbursts at the top. I snap a picture with my phone, then hold it up to show my friends. "This is the ninth sigil of Inanna," I tell them. "The one I'll use today."

♒

Just past noon on the first of August—the Sabbat of Lammas in Wiccan traditions—five magicians walk down the outside steps of an old house on Dumas Street and march toward the Bridge of Lions. The day is blazing hot, high summer in northeast Florida, the air thick and humid under a deep blue sky. Towering white clouds float in from the Atlantic.

We're an unlikely collection of humans: three girls in their early twenties, dressed in shorts, T-shirts, and sandals; one guy, slightly older, in a tank top and baseball cap; a slim Black man in his sixties, in dress slacks and button-down shirt, wearing sunglasses and a wide-brimmed straw hat. But I believe the formula of concealment that we cast must be working. People we pass on the street don't seem to notice us. Even when we turn onto Avenida Menendez, where there are more pedestrians and a constant stream of cars, we draw no curious glances—hardly any glances at all.

So far, so good.

But, two blocks from the bridge, a breeze tickles my earlobe and I let out a gasp. The demon whispers to me, warm stinking breath, laughing, scornful tone. "Oh, you are making a fool of yourself, Abby Renshaw."

When I ignore him, he goes on, "Do you really think you can damage me with a *public* ritual? Too much distraction, too many passing mental influences. This will never work. In fact, it will be funny to watch."

I don't answer, just lift my chin and keep walking.

We cross at the stoplight and enter the narrow park that runs along the waterfront. At the base of the bridge, white marble lions stand on either side of the road. I choose a spot nearby, a patch of lawn between two sidewalks. One of these is straight and runs along the water, where the marina lies packed with boats riding at anchor. The other path winds among cabbage palms and ferns, leading to benches and a white brick pavilion.

Everyone agrees this spot feels as good as any. And I'm comforted by the closeness of the lions. They remind me of Inanna.

After verifying the compass points, we arrange ourselves in a circle. Canary stands in the south, Molly in the east. Ariel is stationed in the west, and Kevin in the north, his back to the cars and trucks driving onto and off the bridge. The traffic noise is not too bad, and only a few people walk by. A woman passes with a Scottish Terrier on a lease. The dog glances at us curiously, the owner not at all.

We pull out our phones and begin.

I decided at the last minute to leave my wand at home—again to be less conspicuous. Instead, I use two fingers to draw the circle of protection around us, instructing my friends to visualize it as a ring of blue fire.

Standing in the center, I extend my arms. "Now we see the ring expand into a sphere, luminous and pure. This energy protects us from evil power and all interference of the mundane world."

My gaze travels around the circle. The faces are calm, watching me. Letting my eyes unfocus, I tap into my spirit vision. Just beyond my friends' backs, I glimpse the energy sphere, vibrating.

And beyond that, something else: a dark orange cloud that writhes and twists and flickers, here and there, into the face of Alyas. The face is huge and angry.

He's not laughing now. As I suspected, his bravado before was an act. He's not sure what to expect.

Good.

Ignoring him, I proceed: "Now, my friends on the path of true magic, we state our intention. We will invoke the great Goddess Inanna, ageless and powerful, and we will then channel her power to summon, bind, and finally banish the evil spirit known as Alyas, who has haunted this place for centuries—but after today will haunt it no more."

Swiping on my phone, I bring up the summons to Inanna and read it in my strongest voice: "Hail to the Lady who lights the morning sky! We call you Inanna, daughter of heaven. You who journey from the Great Above to the Great Below. Come to us now, O

Goddess. Invest us with your power, that we may vanquish an evil being from this earth."

With that, I begin the chant that we've practiced, and the four voices join me:

> By this light,
> In this hour,
> From each realm,
> Send your power.

I pause just an instant to glance around the circle. Everyone is chanting, staring at the sigils on their screens, focusing on those images, investing them with attention and the power of the chant, so that Inanna's spirit will flow into the circle.

Gazing at the phone in my hand I focus on the *Mace of Rulership*. Chanting and chanting, I feel the power grow, until the sigil on my screen shifts and floats into the air, becoming three-dimensional, turning into the actual mace of power that Inanna showed me in the vision. Then I see her standing beside me, holding the mace, beaming with light.

My arms shoot up to stop the chant.

"The presence of the goddess has been summoned," I tell the group. "She is with us. Now we can direct her power to summon and then banish the demon."

Around the circle, the magicians stare back at me, faces alight and eager. Beside me, in the spirit realm, stands Inanna. I point down at the earth.

"Alyas: demon of the place of slaughter. I summon you to this place and time, you who have haunted this city for centuries. By the power of the Goddess Inanna, far older and stronger than you, I compel you now to come into this place, into this circle and be bound. This is the game I promised you."

The others join me in the second chant.

Alyas, by your true name,
We summon you to end the game.

The orange cloud no longer writhes outside the protective sphere. But, as the chant continues, I see an orange funnel, spiraling as it rises out of the ground. I don't know if the others can see the demon, but I sure do—huge, bulky, snarling, hideous.

"Foolish mortals," he bellows. "This will never work. I am older and stronger than all of you together."

I also see Inanna, still standing calmly at my side. I raise my hand in her direction. "But she is older and stronger than you!"

We move on to the final verses:

By this light, in this hour,
We banish you and drain your power.
By this light, from this shore,
We banish you forevermore.

The demon looms taller, laughing a harsh, ferocious laugh.

The fabric of reality shreds in my mind. I still see the circle of magicians, still hear their chanting voices and my own. But mixed with all that, as if on a separate screen, I see Alyas slide into a mist.

His face appears, whispering to my companions, one by one.

First it's Ariel. I hear the demon's voice as if he speaks to me. "This will never work. You tried such nonsense before, and it made you sick, so sick you nearly died ..."

That did happen, my first year at college. We did a ritual by the campus pond to try to banish the frog entity. It backfired badly, and Ariel ended up in the hospital.

Alyas is trying to disrupt our circle. He knows that if he can break one link, the whole thing will snap like a shorted electric circuit.

Ariel blinks, looks scared for a moment. Then he shakes himself and resumes chanting, louder than ever.

By this light, in this hour,
We banish you and drain your power.

The demon tries Molly next, sneering at her, reminding her of her self-doubts, her secret fears of missing out on things, on not being good enough. Molly looks startled. But after a moment she turns in the direction of the demon's voice and laughs out loud.

"Get out of town!" she yells.

Alyas moves on to Kevin, seeking to leverage his grief over losing his life partner, his uncertainty of how he will go on. Kevin's face turns grim. But then he straightens up, still chanting without a pause.

Next, I see the demon at Canary's ear. "You know this is doomed to fail," he whispers. "You know you are doomed. Magic is a fraud. Your whole life is a fraud. You will hate yourself for even trying this. You will walk to the top of that bridge and throw yourself off, ending the fraud forever."

More than the others, Canary looks uncertain and scared. Her voice falters. She glances around like she wants to run.

If she goes, it will break the circle.

I have to stop her, help her. *But how?*

Beside me, Inanna stirs. A beam of gold light flows across the air and touches Canary's heart. The girl's face shows a shock of recognition.

After a moment, she turns to Alyas. "That's no good, demon boy. I am a witch and a daughter of witches. You have no power over me!"

She chants again, the current of the circle restored.

"Agghh!" Alyas howls in frustration and rage.

He slides back to the center, back to me. He should be desperate now, weakened.

But he doesn't look it.

Instead, he grows huge, horns poking the top of the blue sphere, eyes glaring down at me, wicked mouth grinning.

"You've done very well, Abby Renshaw. But all of this has just given me more power to absorb. Now watch, as *I* end the game."

Has he really taken in all of the circle's energy? It can't be …

Or can it?

His enormous hands thrust me down. My spine is jolted and something in my head explodes.

Once more, I'm in the Great Below, kneeling in a stone hall, dank and murky. The demon stands above me, gigantic, laughing.

Despair and terror burn in my heart. I've failed again. I've given Alyas even more power. And this time, there's no escape. This time I'm finished.

The demon's laugh grows louder.

Then it stops.

"Rise, my priestess." Inanna stands beside me, surrounded by an orb of light.

As I'm lifted to my feet, veils part and I glimpse the physical plane—my friends stand in the circle, still chanting, still wielding the sigils.

I'm not alone. Not lost.

Before me, the demon has shrunk to his normal size. He stares around the circle, startled now, frightened.

"Use the Mace of Rulership," Inanna tells me.

In my hand is not my phone, but the actual mace, moon-bladed and lion-headed. I thrust it at the demon. A charge of lightning bursts from the tip.

Two lions formed of fire leap to the ground. Snarling, they pounce on the demon. Alyas stumbles back, a loud, horrible wail ripped from his throat.

Around the circle, I see my fellow magicians, still chanting.

> By this light, from this shore,
> We banish you forevermore.

From the vantage point of the spirit world, I stare in awe as the demon is torn apart by the teeth and claws of Inanna's lions.

And then, from the rips in Alyas' flesh, spirits appear—glowing phantoms of men, women, children—rushing from the demon's wounds. All the people he haunted, I suppose, throughout history. Sighing, groaning, crying with pain or joy or relief, they escape from the demon's body and flow into the sky.

> By this light, in this hour,
> We banish you and drain your power.

The chanting goes on. I glance at the sigil of Inanna's mace, now once again a picture on my phone.

Looking back at the demon, I see that all the trapped spirits have flown away. Alyas' wounds have closed.

And his body has shrunk. He stands at my feet, a hideous orange goblin, inches high and shrinking still.

> By this light, from this shore,
> We banish you forevermore.

With a last glance full of hate, the demon shrivels away to nothing.

〰〰

I stop chanting, and so do the others.

We all look around the circle. Everything is quiet, except for the breeze off the water and the rolling of traffic near the bridge. A seagull caws as it flies overhead.

"Wow," Canary Greene says. "That was the best magic ever."

"Everyone tell me what you saw," Molly cries with excitement.

With psychic events, even practiced magicians are liable to see things differently. In this case, all of us saw some image of the demon, and everyone heard, or felt, him speaking to them individually, trying to weaken their resolve.

"I saw ghosts breaking out of his body," Molly exclaims. "Did anyone else?"

"Yes," Canary answers. "And flying away. I think they were the spirits of people he had trapped."

"Spirits, or just trapped energy," Kevin surmises. "I've never seen anything like it."

"And did you see the demon shrink and then vanish?" Molly asks.

"Yes," Canary says. "When the trapped energy left him, he got small. So tiny. And then he was gone."

"He *is* gone," I answer, feeling it definitely. "Thanks to all of you."

Molly comes over and rests a hand on my shoulder. "Way to go, Abby. And you're okay?"

"Yeah," I reply after thinking it over. "Good. Really good."

Molly grins. "Well, I guess we're done here. Who wants lunch?"

"Okay," I answer. "But I'm buying."

25. Table for five, please

Barnacles is crowded at lunchtime, so we have to wait for a table. While we stand in line, several of the staff recognize Canary and come over to greet her.

"Good to see you, Cary," one of them says. "You coming back to work here?"

Canary smiles. "Maybe. Right now, anything seems possible."

We get a table near the window and are able to drink in the spectacular view. St. Augustine is a beautiful place, and it really is a gorgeous day. Canary mentions that part of her Wiccan tradition is to follow up a ritual with a feast. We make sure our lunch fits that description: seafood, salads, French fries, plenty of fresh bread. Ariel orders a beer and the rest of drink iced tea or lemonade.

"You know," Molly says, "that sigil magic is pretty amazing. But now that I've seen how powerful it can be, I'm really not sure about writing the book."

"Why not?" I ask her.

Molly sighs. "Not sure we can do the subject justice. Also, not sure how much of it we *should* be sharing publicly. You know how the Circle of Harmony texts say, over and over, 'These things are secret and not to be taken lightly.' I'm starting to see why that can be true."

I nod, and glance over at Kevin, who is also nodding, a slight smile on his lips.

"Also," Molly says, "I have all that historical material on Harmony Springs and the Circle, and its different offshoots, and people who came and studied for just a short time but had fascinating lives and experiences in other places. There's more than enough research there to keep me busy for years. I think I ought to focus on that if I'm really going to publish it eventually. I mean, focus on that along with college and work and all … I do hope you'll continue to work with me on the history, Abby, when you have time."

"Of course I will."

"You know," Kevin says, "if you can stand having a retired academic put his hand in, I wouldn't mind contributing."

Molly's eyes go wide. "Are you *kidding*? Kevin, I would *love* to have your help. That would be so awesome."

Ariel lifts his beer glass. "I look forward to reading your chronicles," he says cheerfully. "I'm more convinced than ever that I really need to resume my magical studies."

"Me too," Canary says. "After today, I'd like to learn more about this Circle of Harmony."

~~~

After our pleasant and leisurely feast, we walk back along the Avenida, across the city plaza, and through the south side of the historic district. By the time we reach my house on Dumas Street, it's nearly 3:30.

Hugs are exchanged all around. Molly and Kevin climb into his old RAV and start back for Harmony Springs. Canary drives off to return her mother's car to Lake Sylvan.

Ariel lingers. Standing on the sidewalk, we look into each other's eyes. Smiling, he takes my hand.

"Always great to see you, Abby. I'm so glad I could help you today—and that you called on me."

His hand feels so good touching mine.

Sometimes I'm impulsive, and this is one of those times.

"Come with me?"

Still holding hands, I lead him up the driveway and the stairs. Inside the apartment, I shut the door, and then I kiss him, long and hard.

Maybe it's partly the energy of Inanna still inside me. She is, among other things, a goddess of love. Maybe it's just that I love Ariel, and desire him, and at this moment all my obstructions and hesitations have disappeared.

"Can you stay a little longer," I ask, breathless, hugging him tight.

He shakes with a laugh. "What do you think?"

〰️

Later, arm in arm, we walk back to his car. He's told me he'd like to stay longer, but it's an hour and a half back to Orlando, and he has to catch up on all of today's work that he's missed—and be at work tomorrow. I told him I totally understand.

This makes me think we need to be clear about expectations.

Standing beside his car, feeling awkward, I broach the subject. "This was wonderful. And, like I said, I love you. But, we haven't talked about where we go from here. I mean, where this might lead ..."

"Where do you want it to lead?"

"Well, I don't want it to end, that's for sure. I'll be in Harmony Springs one more year, and you'll be in Orlando. Hopefully, we can visit each other?"

"Often, I should think."

"Great. But then, I may be moving up north next year. Or, I expect I'll definitely be going to law school someplace. I just have so much to think about. And I know you have plans too ..." I catch his expression, fond but amused. "Am I thinking too far ahead on this?"

He laughs, takes me in his arms. "Include me in your thinking, and I'll include you in mine."

〰️

Sunday morning, almost two weeks since our circle at the Bridge of Lions, I wake up early. Ariel's still asleep in my bed. The fact that it's a single bed means we have to sleep close together, but neither of us minds. Guess that's how it works when you're in love.

Ariel's told me he doesn't want to run this morning. He's tired, having worked most of yesterday, even though it was Saturday, then driven up from Orlando to be with me. So, careful not to wake him, I duck into the bathroom to change into my running clothes.

Being with Ariel feels so good. I've never felt so close to another person—so much trust, so much joy. Last weekend, despite the mountain of work I had to catch up on for the office, I drove to Orlando for a day to be with him. A relationship should be a two-way street.

Now, I tiptoe to the door and exit as quietly as I can.

After warm-up exercises at the base of the steps, I start off. My physical energy has come back nicely. This past week, I ran almost every morning, and I'm starting to build up my fitness again. The cut on my wrist is also healing, the remains of the stitches not nearly so gross as they once were. I guess the barbed white line will never go away entirely.

But, hey, I've got other scars. I can cope.

Speaking of ugly marks, I heard from Jeremy the day after we banished the demon. He texted me and begged to talk. Thinking I might regret it later, I gave in to my curiosity and called him. Turned out, he was no longer terrified or suicidal, only hazy and confused.

"I don't understand what happened," he babbled.

"Why? Because your demon friend is gone?"

"Not only that, the game is gone. I mean, all the code is still there, but when I start it up, all the life has vanished. It's just like some half-assed arcade game now: flat, uninteresting. I thought I was gaining all of this ... feeling and power. But the demon took it all away. Now, my whole life feels like the game, dull, pointless."

"Well, I can promise you, the demon's not coming back."

"Oh, I don't want him back. Only ..."

"You want my advice?"

"Sure."

"Go for a walk. Go to the beach. Go out to a bar and have a drink. Talk to people. Try to remember you're part of the human race."

"Huh ..."

Jeremy might have actually been ready to take my advice. Not sure. Happily, he's not my problem anymore.

I cross King Street east of the plaza, jog past Flagler College and the big church on the corner. At this early hour, the north side of the historic district is quiet, cars parked on the narrow brick streets, well-kept old houses. I pass the Office of Sheldon and Bond, where I'll be back at work tomorrow morning.

Two weeks left on my internship. Since the day after we booted out the demon, I've worked extremely hard at the office. First, I made it a point to meet separately with both Larry and Teresa and apologize for all the missed time. Without going into detail, I promised that the issues causing my absences had been resolved. Since then, I've been focused and super diligent, "going the extra mile," as Larry likes to say. I've also asked both attorneys for their advice on applying to law schools—and dropped subtle and not-so-subtle hints that I hope they'll both write me positive recommendations.

Running east now, toward the old Spanish fort and the water.

As for law school applications, given my returning energy and the total lack of demon distractions, I've also managed time for researching my options. And, I have to admit, the more I look, the more those two schools in New York seem the best options for environmental law. So I've about decided to apply to both Pace and NYU. Mom will be pleased. Of course, I'll cover my bets and apply to Miami and UF too.

Coming in sight of the river, I think about how much I love Florida, how I really don't want to leave, even for a few years.

And what about my relationship with Ariel? Can it last if I'm mostly out-of-state? Maybe, once I get my degree and pass the bar, I can find work with a practice in Orlando. Ariel and I could become life partners, maybe even get married …

Okay, I'm thinking *way* too far ahead. I need to enjoy our love now and be grateful, and deal with the changes as they come.

I run south along the avenue, cross at the traffic light, and trot up the sidewalk onto the Bridge of Lions. It's all so lovely in the morning light. I want to take a good look at the water.

Besides Ariel, there are other reasons I'm hesitant to leave Florida—Grandma and my friends in Harmony Springs. Naturally, I would visit as often as possible. Still, separating from them and my life there would be painful. Don't really want to think about that.

Except, I have to …

Reaching the top of the bridge, I stop to catch my breath. Gazing around, I appreciate the soft breeze, the sparkling water, the stunning beauty. I think of our circle, and how my friends helped me banish the demon. I think of the Goddess Inanna and all the spiritual gifts she's given me.

Despite the uncertainty of my future, I am so happy.

And there are *some* things I'm sure of. Wherever I end up going to law school, I will bring the Circle of Harmony and my magical tools with me. I will bring Inanna with me.

And, a year and a day from last July 30th, I will walk to the top of Bliss Spring and summon Lebab. And I will pledge to him know that, as long as I live, I will always do my best to protect the Springs of Harmony.

Author's Note

Abby's adventures are told in long stories and short. The ones published to date are:

- Ghosts of Bliss Bayou (novel)
- Ghosts of Tamgrove Hall (novella)
- Ghosts of Lock Tower (novel)
- Ghosts of Prosper Key (novella)
- Ghosts of the Mermaid Spring (novella)
- A Demon on the Lion Bridge

These stories take place in a mix of actual and fictional locations. In the present book, Harmony Springs and Lake Sylvan are fictional, while Jacksonville and (I'm told) Orlando are real. St. Augustine is not only real, but its neighborhoods, environs, and history are portrayed as authentically as possible. It really is a beautiful place, and you should visit if you ever have the chance.

I'm very grateful to my beta readers: Marilyn Massa, John W. Kelly, and Vicki-Marie Petrick, as well as to my cover artist, Shaun Stevens of Flintlock Covers (www.flintlockcovers.com).

Thank you for reading *A Demon on the Lion Bridge*. I sincerely hope you enjoyed it. Please consider posting an honest rating and review on Amazon, as well as other sites.

Also by Jack Massa

The Glimnodd Cycle - epic fantasy in a world of witches and pirates.
Cloak of the Two Winds
A Mirror Against All Mishap
Tournament of Witches
Witches of Glimnodd (the Complete Collection)

A Conjurer of Rhodes - historical fantasy set in the ancient world.
The Mazes of Magic
The Lights of Alexandria
The Treasure of the Sun God

I love hearing from readers! You can connect with me at
Web: triskelionbooks.com or jackmassa.com
Facebook: Facebook.com/AuthorJackMassa/
Twitter: @JackMassa2